The King's Gambit

a novel by

Tom Blenk

authorHOUSE®

AuthorHouse™
1663 Liberty Drive, Suite 200
Bloomington, IN 47403
www.authorhouse.com
Phone: 1-800-839-8640

First published by AuthorHouse   7/14/2009

ISBN: 978-1-4389-3756-4 (sc)
ISBN: 978-1-4389-3757-1 (hc)

Printed in the United States of America
Bloomington, Indiana

This book is printed on acid-free paper.

This book is dedicated to the memory of my father

Robert Gerard Blenk

"An Uncommon Man"

"THE KING'S GAMBIT"

gam'bit (gam'bit) *n* [F., f. Pr. *cambi* an exchange.] 1. A chess move or series of moves in which the first player offers to sacrifice a piece for an opponent's piece to gain advantage in position.

FOREWORD

L ong before the "Boys of Winter" skated to immortality in the
1980 Winter Olympics, a solo American ended the Soviet
Union's dominance in a worldwide competition. In the
summer of 1972, in Reykjavik, Iceland, a young American named
Bobby Fischer accomplished what many thought was impossible.
He handily beat long time defending World Champion Boris
Spassky in the World Chess Championship. The Russians
dominated the world of chess for more than a half century, and
Spassky was the latest in the Soviet's long line of world champion
grandmasters. Solid, stoic, and relentless at the table, he calculated
every move and never made a serious blunder. No one ever rattled
him.

Fischer was no slouch. Though he had never done well in
the qualifying tournaments, he dominated a who's who of former
world champions and grand masters in the 1972 qualifiers. Fischer
was young, eccentric and brilliant, but he had never even won
a game against the great Spassky. Most experts expected the
Russian to win again.

The match drew worldwide attention. People who rarely, or
never, played chess, tuned in on a nightly basis to watch chess
expert Shelby Lyman move pieces on an over-sized black and white
board, as cross-Atlantic calls delivered Fischer's and Spassky's every
move. Newspapers, most notably *The New York Times*, allocated
daily columns describing each match in detail. In the heart of
The Cold War, with the race to the moon decided and the arms

race in full swing, it became more than a chess game. The match became the United States versus the Soviet Union. Capitalism versus Communism. Freedom versus Imperialism. The whole world was watching.

After losing game one and forfeiting game two, Fischer dominated the rest of the match, winning five and tying three of the next eight games. With each passing day, between July 11th and September 1st, the world became more and more fascinated with the idea that young American Bobby Fischer was about to end the Russian stranglehold on the world of chess. The game of chess had entered the mainstream.

In his final column on the event, Richard Roberts of *The New York Times* wrote:

"The world of chess suddenly found itself moved into the main arena on almost an equal billing with great political and social events. Never again would tournaments, matches, and Olympiads go back to the dim world of semi-oblivion they had long endured."

PROLOGUE

*"From the moment you start to play, the smallest error
can be fatal in a top level game of chess."*

Shelby Lyman

The long winding access road off highway 395 in Uncasville, Connecticut seems never-ending. The feeling is magnified by the anticipation, or anxiety, of every motorist seeking fun, food, romance, relaxation, and riches—especially riches, because in reality, no one goes to a casino without thoughts of winning.

Suddenly, the Mohegan Sun Resort rises majestically out of the darkness like Atlantis rising from the sea. The casino hotel sits in a valley of bright lights and huge structures surrounded by parking lots and garages, absorbing streams of cars like giant sponges, leaving only a trickle of traffic moving away and into the night. Casino parking is rarely a problem due to the constant turnover of winners and losers leaving in various degrees of happiness and despair.

Winter, summer, and autumn denote the three main access points for patrons entering the resort. Floor to ceiling glass doors open onto marble floors leading to The Casino of the Earth and The Casino of the Sky. These two main gaming rooms flank the Mohegan Sun Arena which serves as the ground floor of the resort's thirty-four story luxury hotel.

A cavalcade of shops featuring everything from autographed nostalgia to Indian artwork, line both sides of the giant foyer that stretches from The Earth to The Sky. Eat in elegance at Michael Jordan's, or catch a burger at Johnny Rocket's Malt Shop. The choices for shopping and food along this corridor are as endless as the crowd that constantly flows back and forth across the Waterfall Bridge, from one end of the resort to the other.

In the middle of all this stands the most prominent and unique piece of art at the resort. Patrons stare at it, point at it, argue about what it is, but most importantly they use it for a point of reference or place to rendezvous. The blown glass structure of blue, green and white stands ten feet tall. It rises above a wishing well and stands in front of the majestic stone waterfall adorning the wall above Tuscany's Restaurant.

This magnificent sculpture may represent just a splash in a well or a tempest over the ocean, but at 11:58 p.m., all it meant to the tall man dressed in black slacks and gold vest, was a halfway point between the break room and his table. Blackjack dealers get twenty minutes, and Michael was due back at midnight.

He glanced at his watch as he glided through the crowd, turning a hip or shoulder just enough to avoid contact, without breaking stride. "Two minutes, perfect," he breathed to himself. He was cutting it close. Exactly as planned.

The pit bosses hated him and Hank would be worried as usual. Hank would be watching and waiting, wondering if, this time, his best dealer would be late. They were morons. He would never be late. He was just practicing. Precision and timing are the keys to the success of any plan, and his plan was about to become reality. After fourteen years, the time was almost at hand. Michael Mueller squeezed by Hank and tapped his relief on the shoulder. His watch read 11:59:58.

* * *

Kim Soo perched, more than sat, her hundred pound frame on a small wooden chair in the corner of her hotel room. With knees under her chin and arms wrapped around her shins, she stared through the dim light filtering from the edges of the curtains. The Stradivarius gleamed from the open violin case on the glass tabletop. Her parents sold and mortgaged all they had to find this piece of history, and give her talent every opportunity to succeed. From the age of six, her ability was unquestioned. Once in her hands, nothing in life existed beyond the mahogany sheen of the two hundred-year-old instrument. When she played, the violin became a part of her. It became a fifth appendage or a second soul, thinking and feeling the same thoughts and emotions with no conscious effort on her part. From the beginning, the talent was unmistakable. The family became musical nomads traveling throughout Asia and Europe, moving from teaching maestros, to recitals, to concerts. They had sacrificed their lives for her. Through it all she made one promise, to take her talent as far as she could. No matter the sacrifice, she vowed to repay them by reaching the pinnacle of being the greatest concert violinist of her time, if not of all time.

Now the eighteen-year old beauty could not bring herself to touch the violin. She could not talk to her parents. They would not even understand. All she had to do was say yes, and she could step on the stage at Carnegie Hall as first violin for The New York Philharmonic Orchestra on the night of its triumphant return to the great concert hall. Kim Soo could not believe the last twenty-four hours. The ultimate high of a private session with the renowned conductor Vincent Antonelli, followed by a dinner invitation to discuss her future, had been trampled by his disgusting proposal. He made it clear she could fulfill her dream on stage, but she would have to perform in a very different way for him.

Her promise pounded in her head. No matter what the sacrifice. Softly crying, she buried her head on her knees.

* * *

The young blackjack dealer waited patiently. Much more so than the other six players sitting in various degrees of anticipation at his table. Two Asian men chain smoked and chattered incessantly in a maddening combination of their native tongue and broken English. They were self professed experts on the game of blackjack and spent most of their time criticizing the other players and shuffling their chips. Three brothers from New Jersey occupied the other end of the table. They were in the midst of a four day drunken bachelor party, and really didn't care what anyone had to say about how they played their cards, especially the two dudes opposite them. In the middle sat the object of everyone's attention: Gramps and his wife. Gramps had to be seventy if he was a day, and he might get to eighty by the time he made his decision. Michael let a little smile play at the corners of his mouth. It never ceased to amaze him how hard people worked to try and beat the game of blackjack. He wanted to scream "luck and percentages." Play the percentages and hope for some luck. There is no more to it, you can't outsmart the cards. It is a simple game. What do you have? What does the dealer have, and should you take a card? If the dealer has six or less showing, and you have twelve or more, don't take a card. If the dealer has seven or more showing, and you have 16 or less, take a card. It is that simple with a few variations.

Gramps' situation screamed out for one of these variations. "Double down." Double your bet and hope the one card you get is a ten and that the dealer will bust. Gramps had the six of diamonds and the four of spades, adding up to ten. The dealer showed the five of spades.

"What do you think, son?" Gramps asked.

"I'm sorry, sir, I'm not allowed to sway your decision," he replied.

"No braina! No braina! Ol' man. You dubba down. Go!" Asian number one prodded.

The dealer's smile disappeared as Gramps made his bet. Staring down the Asian loud mouth, he turned up the next card to Gramps. Five of hearts. Fifteen, not good for Gramps. He turned up his hole card. A ten of spades, also giving him fifteen. In Blackjack the dealer must take a card on anything below seventeen and must stay on seventeen or more. The ace of spades followed by the five of diamonds put the dealer on twenty one exactly, drawing an array of muttering, groaning and swearing from everyone at the table. The anguished "Oh no!" from Gramps caught at Michael for a second, but only for a second, he had no time for sentiment. These people had no idea what a real game was. A game of intelligence and strategy where every move is scrutinized by the whole world. His game. His recreation. His legacy. He glanced at his watch again. This time he looked for the date: July 10th. Soon, he thought. Just one more day.

* * *

Carnegie Hall officially opened its doors on May 5th, 1891, in a five day musical extravaganza never before seen in the United States, and maybe not seen anywhere in the world. After arriving in their ornate horse drawn carriages, and armed with their $1 or $2 box seat tickets, the audience settled in to an evening unmatched in artistic splendor and luxury. The on-stage talent featured twenty-nine year old Walter Damrosch leading the Symphony Society of New York in an opening rendition of Beethoven's Overture No. 3, followed by famed Russian composer Pyotr Tchaikovsky conducting his own composition of Marche, solemnly. But the next day's critical reviews and gossip concentrated on the new Music Hall itself, and the incredible sound it generated.

Many experts believed the unique architecture of the building was directly responsible for the extraordinary acoustics in the main hall. Architect William Burnet Tuthill used a Guastavino process in the construction of Carnegie Hall, which called for thick walls of masonry and concrete instead of steel beams. The sound generated by the main hall prompted the renowned artist and benefactor Isaac Stern to comment, "It has been said that the hall itself is an instrument."

Vincent Antonelli stood in the front row of the fifth tier of seats, one hundred and five steps above the main floor, looking down on the stage where he would lead The New York Philharmonic Orchestra in its triumphant return to Carnegie Hall. The Philharmonic and The Symphony Society of New York merged in 1928 to form The New York Philharmonic and spent the next seventy years headlining the main room at Carnegie Hall. In 1962, the orchestra moved to Philharmonic Hall, later moving to Avery Fisher Hall, at Lincoln Center. Today, the New York Philharmonic performs more than one hundred eighty times a year, mostly at Lincoln Center, during their September to June subscription season. Vincent Antonelli followed a prestigious list of conductors to lead The New York Philharmonic. From Damrosch and Tchaikovsky on opening night, the leaders of the orchestra included the greatest conductors of all time. Mahler, Klemperer, Strauss, Mengelberg, Toscanini, Stravinsky, and Leonard Bernstein all graced the stage as conductors of the most renowned symphony orchestra in the world. Now it was Antonelli's turn. After seven years at the helm, he finally convinced the powers that be to bring the orchestra back to the place it belonged.

On July 13th the New York Philharmonic would return after almost forty-five years, to the most famous music hall in the world, for a season ending gala. At thirty nine, the Italian American protégé had conquered the world of classical music, and held the elite of New York Society in the palm of his hands. No one dared to question his on-stage antics, his brutal criticism of individual orchestra members, or the veiled accusations of certain former female employees. In the eyes of the experts, Vincent Antonelli stood with the great conductors of all time. His reputation on stage forgave what they considered to be his minor foibles.

Antonelli moved slowly down the four flights to the corridor behind the box seats, above the main mezzanine. He unlocked the door to the private box centered above the stage in the Main Hall. He knew every inch of the small ornate room, from the rich burgundy rugs and wall coverings, to the gold railings and overstuffed chairs. This was Andrew Carnegie's private box. Here, he and his young wife, Louise, watched every concert. Vincent spent every evening relaxing in the darkness of Box Thirty-Three after each rehearsal. It was here that he would wait for young Kim Soo to make her decision. What else could she do, he thought, First Violin for this orchestra, in this format, at her age. No. She would have to give in. It was the chance of a lifetime.

Vincent Antonelli unbuttoned his coat and sat with his feet on the rail facing the stage. He smiled an evil grin.

Power is so intoxicating, he thought.

* * *

Michael filled his lungs slowly, then released. Eyes closed trying to ease his racing heartbeat he let his arms hang to the floor on either side of the padded bench. The intense hour and fifteen minute workout always ended with a maximum bench press. A three mile, half hour run on the treadmill followed by fifteen high-speed minutes on the Stair Master began his daily workout. Then, a half hour of free weights, which ended today with thirty reps at one hundred and thirty-five pounds, completed the task.

Dragging himself off the bench, he stripped the soaked t-shirt and gym shorts off and threw them in the laundry basket in the corner. The room was small, but comfortable. A queen-sized bed with matching dresser and night stand were the only furniture in the room. He stood in the middle of the circular braided rug and surveyed his naked body in the full length wall mirror. His lean muscular body glistened and rippled with each move, and he felt and saw his arousal growing. Turning away, he headed for the shower. He would not give into any weakness with the game so close. It had been a long day followed by a three hour trip home, an hour and twenty minutes spent on the Cross Sound Ferry from New London to Orient Point. Driving to Greenport and island-hopping the two mini ferries across to Sag Harbor, always took its toll on him. He was thankful that his mother was out, probably bowling or playing bridge with her cronies. He had grabbed a bottle of water and headed straight for his room. Two hours later, tired from the workout and comforted by the hot shower, he crawled under the covers to sleep, hoping this time the dream would not come.

* * *

GAME 1

July 11th

"When the first pieces begin to move out on each side, a precarious situation is immediately created. You can't relax your attention for a moment."

Shelby Lyman

T he young boy's smile filled the room. *Master will be so proud. Only great players make such bold moves in such a crucial moment.*

"Sir! Look! Look! I've been so anxious for you to see. Isn't it the most beautiful move?" the young boy pleaded.

"No, Michael. I am very sorry, but you have failed to see far enough ahead. Your king will be in serious jeopardy within six moves and you will be forced to resign. Once again, you are overanxious when you should have played a waiting game. I'm afraid it is a serious blunder," the great Grand Master said, patting the boy on the head.

His water-filled eyes darted to his father sitting hunched over in a small straight back chair, watching the board intently. He watched his father's pleading eyes climb to match the Grand Master's steely gaze.

"I am sorry," the Master said "but the boy will never be the player you dreamed of, Sir. He is very gifted, but not a candidate for Grand Master or even national competition. You are wasting your money. You must stop for the sake of the boy and yourself."

The dejected Jefferson Mueller dropped his head to his hands as the young boy heard the Grand Master's final words pounding over and over in his mind.

"I cannot waste any more of my valuable time on Michael."

"Waste time on Michael."

"Waste time Michael"

"Michael."

His eyes snapped open. He was soaked in sweat, pulse racing again, but he was awake. So why was the Master still calling his name?

It was his mother's voice.

"You left a note for me to wake you at 5 a.m.," she said, with a soft knock on his door.

"Thanks, Mother, I'm up," he replied.

He was in his own bed safe from the dream again. A dream, yes, but he knew it had really happened, and he could not go back and fix it. But he could prove them wrong. The Master and everyone else would see how far he could go, and Father would once again be proud. He hopped out of bed and headed for the bathroom. He had a train to catch at 6:22.

* * *

The Long Island Railroad streams from the tips of the Island's two fingers to the heart of New York City like blood running through the human body. The lifeline of the greatest city in the world brings almost three hundred thousand commuters daily and over eighty-five million people a year from the outer reaches of the Island to New York's five boroughs. The train's tentacles reach from towns like Montauk, Hampton Bays, Ronkonkoma and Bellport, through as many as thirty stops on the two to three hour commute. The blue, green, and red lines snake westward, accepting and deleting patrons on platforms in Islip, Babylon, and Hicksville, converging on the Jamaica transfer station. From Jamaica, it is a short trip to the main terminals at Flatbush Avenue in Brooklyn and Penn Station in Manhattan.

On trips to the city, Michael never left the house on the quaint residential street in Sag Harbor empty-handed. Garment bag, rolling suitcase, cooler, and duffel bag all lined the wall in his bedroom. Today he carried a black knapsack over his shoulder filled with two complete changes of clothes. This time he would not be returning to the house in Sag Harbor. His first transformation would come in the bathroom of a 7-Eleven or gas station before he reached the Southampton train station. He would enter as a student and leave as a businessman on his way to a high paying job on Wall Street.

He arrived at the train station fifteen minutes early. The idea, as always, was to blend in. Too early could lead to familiarity with other commuters. Too late, running for the train, would make him conspicuous. Complete with I-pod, headphones, and a Yankees cap worn backwards, the young student took a seat in a middle car and opened an American History textbook. Inside the textbook he opened the L.I.R.R. train schedule. He made his decision quickly. Bay Shore would serve as the site of his next transition.

The sites changed on each trip to and from the city, but the results never did. Entering the terminal restroom as a construction worker, businessman, or college student, Michael always left as stock broker Frank Lewitzky. Frank Lewitzky looked much different than the slouching, shoe-scuffling student that had disembarked from the train. Touches of gray in the wig, and the classic black slacks and sweater, topped with a dark suit coat, gave Michael the look of serious businessman Frank Lewitzky. He took a seat in a different car and began sifting through papers retrieved from the leather briefcase on his lap.

The train arrived at Penn Station at 8:42 a.m. Lewitzky followed the crowd through the terminal to the Red Line which would take him to the Upper West Side of Manhattan. Always the subway instead of the bus. More people. More shadows. Less chance of being noticed.

Lewitzky rose from the subway at the intersection of Broadway, Eighth Avenue, and Central Park South. He walked briskly four blocks up Central Park West, turning left on Sixty-Fourth Street. The narrow tree-lined street had a definite upscale feeling. Rows of brownstone apartment buildings with black wrought iron fences and gates bordered the cobblestone sidewalks. Reaching the third building on his right, Lewitzky took the front steps two at a time, reached the foyer, and walked the two flights up to his apartment. Inside the apartment Lewitzky became Michael Mueller once again.

The six room apartment was furnished in a restored Victorian décor, with a sunken living room, master bedroom, guest bedroom, kitchen, and two baths. Michael stepped down from the marble entrance, crossed the hardwood floor and Persian rug and headed straight into the master bedroom. Striding around the rustic iron sleigh bed, Mueller pressed a small red button behind the night stand. The vertical lines in the wallpaper design disappeared as the wall between the corner and the bed slid left into a hidden recessed wall pocket. He stepped into the panic room, switched on the light and closed the door behind him.

Bobby Fischer's life-sized poster stared at him from the far wall.

A thrill of anticipation ran down his spine. The planning was over. Tonight he would make his opening move.

He slipped on a pair of rubber gloves from his pocket and opened the door to the first of ten lockers lining the right hand wall. From inside he retrieved a change of clothes, a digital camera, and a small black knapsack. Twenty minutes later, he was ready. Checking the contents of the knapsack, he walked to a large slanted easel that dominated the center of the room. Small zip-lock bags were arranged in the top left hand corner numbered one through ten. He took the bag marked "one," put it in the front pocket of the knapsack, stepped back into the bedroom, and closed the panic room door.

Five minutes later, an older looking man left by the back entrance of Frank Lewitzky's brownstone looking exactly like every other tourist in New York City.

He bought his ticket and joined the other twenty-five people waiting, in the ornate entrance to Carnegie Hall, for the tour to begin. Michael had transformed himself into an older, balding guy wearing a Red Sox baseball cap, a brand new NYC t-shirt, a pair of khaki shorts and black Nike running shoes.

* * *

Vincent Antonelli twirled the ornate baton in his nimble fingers with the ease of an expert drum major. The twelve inch spiked ivory instrument, with an ebony handle, gleamed in the harsh light of his dressing table. He turned the handle to read his name engraved in gold. *Yes, I will bring this along tonight. I will use whatever it takes to convince her.* His mood was electric in anticipation.

Rehearsals were going splendidly, but Vincent Antonelli would never let his orchestra know he was pleased. The violin section took the brunt of his criticism today. Just two days away from the concert, Regina had to know her seat as First Chair was in jeopardy, even if her playing was flawless. Time after time, with looks, gestures or actual public tongue lashings, he invented nonexistent mistakes to the point of threatening to replace her before the big night. Demanding she report to his dressing room following today's rehearsal, he left no doubt about his possible intentions.

"I will not go into this concert with a bumbling first violin. Improve or you will be gone come Sunday night. There is no shortage of young talent waiting in the wings. Now get out of my sight. You have ruined any chance of relaxation on my part."

Vincent laughed as he thought of Regina rushing from his room in tears with no possible way to improve her predicament.

"Power again. I swear it is almost better than sex. Almost, but not if little Kim shows tonight," he whispered to himself.

Quickly he dressed for his conquest. Tonight Kim Soo would make her decision. By night's end she would be in his bed and on this stage two nights later, or she would wallow in obscurity the rest of her violin-playing days. He would see to that. Worst case scenario, Regina would remain in place until he found a new pupil. Vincent locked the baton in its black carrying case and tucked it under his arm. He picked up two wine glasses, a silver carafe filled with ice, and a bottle of Dom Peron. He left his dressing room and headed for Box Thirty-Three.

* * *

Luanda, the small African-American tour guide, was not only highly intelligent and classy, but Michael was sure she had performed in the Great Hall at some point. She had to be sixty years old, but she carried herself like a much younger woman. She led the group through a series of hallways featuring signed photos of nearly every performer and benefactor in Carnegie Hall's history. Luanda continued to spell out the history of the Music Hall during the elevator ride to the upper mezzanine. After relaying everything from Carnegie's first opening to the upcoming return of the Philharmonic, she took them into the Main Hall and down to the stage. The group ended the tour as all tours end at Carnegie Hall, performing as a group in the Great Hall by singing "Happy Birthday" to one of the entourage before exiting through the side entrance to the Carnegie Hall Museum.

Vincent Antonelli listened to the tinny, off-key voices wafting up from the stage. He grinned and leaned back to wait for young Kim Soo. He did not notice that the tour group left with one less tourist than when it entered the hall.

The King's Gambit

* * *

Kim Soo tried to stop shaking while she dressed herself with the clothes carefully laid out on her bed. The lingerie, white, delicate and lacy, hugged her body as she rolled dark hose slowly up her long, slim legs. The young Asian girl stood and caught her image in the mirrored door of the hotel bathroom. Kim Soo sobbed audibly. He would see her like this tonight. He would see even more. He would touch her and she would not stop him. She turned away and quickly finished dressing, pulling a purple silk blouse over her head and zipping her mid-length black skirt around her hips. It was time to go. The decision was made. She would endure this degrading night for her parents. They would never know, and they would be so proud of her success. Kim Soo left her hotel room for Carnegie Hall, determined to keep the promise she made so long ago.

* * *

As Carnegie Hall fell dark and silent, Michael waited calmly in one of the many workshop rooms set aside for concert performers. After slipping away from the tour group, he had made his way here for final preparations to put his game in motion. It was eleven o'clock, and the last workers and visitors were gone. Security amounted to one retired police officer sitting, reading, and dozing in the front entrance box office. He pulled on a pair of coveralls, put his knapsack inside the rolling janitor's wagon, and made his way through the dark hallways to the service elevators.

Vincent Antonelli woke slowly from his catnap to see a tall man in a baseball cap standing over him. Some kind of contraption with brooms, mops, and a trash bucket stood behind the man. He bristled instantly as he smoothed his clothes and sat up straight. "How dare you enter without knocking? Do you know who I am?" He shouted.

The man raised his right hand and sprayed a fine mist from a small plastic aerosol stick into the conductor's face. Antonelli was knocked unconscious instantly. Michael placed the gold leaf black box in his victim's lap and wheeled the swivel chair toward the door.

Twenty minutes later, groggy with the acrid smell of smelling salts in his nose, the young maestro opened cloudy eyes to once again see the strange man intently watching him. Vincent Antonelli's bravado was gone. Something was wrong, very wrong. He could not move. He was tied to a straight back chair against a railing at the top of the flight of stairs leading to the box seat compartments. His arms and legs were taped to the chair with duct tape. His head was pulled back and taped to the railing. Vincent began to panic and sweat profusely.

"What? What do you want? Please don't hurt me! Money? Ok, I am very rich! I know people! Whatever you want," he pleaded.

Michael ignored the terrified conductor. From his bag he took the small plastic baggy and removed a folded piece of paper. In the inside pocket of his victim's jacket, he found the man's billfold and inserted the folded paper into one of the pockets. Returning the billfold to its proper place, he turned his attention to the shaking man strapped to the chair.

He opened the box and removed the baton from its case. Vincent's eyes tried to follow his captor's hands as he brought the pointed instrument to the side of his victim's neck. His finger played along the man's neck until he found his spot. The shocked look on Vincent Antonelli's face froze in place, as the tip of the baton plunged through his jugular, sending a stream of blood spraying across the face of the bronze bust of long-time Carnegie director, Robert Simon.

At six-fifteen in the morning, when Head Custodian Ralph Anderson turned the corner at the top of the stairs, the look on the face of the famed conductor of the New York City Philharmonic had not changed.

The King's Gambit

* * *

Ralph Anderson stumbled into the security office at Carnegie Hall a few minutes before six-thirty, startling Albert Freeman. The sixty-two year old retired patrol officer, who served as the night watchman/security guard, was fidgeting in his favorite swivel chair, thirty-five minutes shy of heading home for a day of celebrating the birth of his new great-grandson, when Ralph crashed into the room. His wife had called in the early morning hours with the big news, and he had thought of little else since. Now, as he dialed 9-1-1, from somewhere deep inside, the instincts from twenty-five years on the force tried to kick into gear. He knew he was setting in motion the best police force in the world.

All 9-1-1 calls go through a civilian operator in Brooklyn. After determining the number and location of the call, the 911 operator rerouted the call with a priority preference. He or she sent the message to the Manhattan 9-1-1 dispatcher for the 18th Precinct at the Midtown North Precinct. At the same time, the call triggered The New York City Fire Department to send paramedics to the scene for an aided case, meaning someone is in need of medical attention. The Manhattan dispatcher's call would also alert a sector car from Midtown North.

* * *

Nicky Walsh loved being a cop. She even loved waiting at the beginning of each shift as Scotty got his coffee and bagel from his favorite deli. Maybe because it was the only time the twenty-year vet let her drive, or just because it gave her a chance to sit and watch the city wake up. Probably both, she thought. She was on the job a year now, and Scotty was finally accepting the fact that a twenty-two year old female, straight out of the Academy, was a pretty good cop. They had worked a lot of jobs together over that time, and had as good an arrest record as any radio motor car

9

in the 18th Precinct. Things had actually been slow lately, which wasn't a bad thing. Nicky smiled, watching Scotty through the window, holding court with everyone inside who would listen, probably giving a play-by-play of his beloved Yankee's win the night before.

The radio static broke the silence in the patrol car.

"17 Adam, respond. Aided case, corner of 57th and 7th. Report subject inside Carnegie Hall. Call in at 06:20 hours. Call from security personnel, Carnegie Hall. FDNY has been notified. Ambulance dispatched."

Nicky instinctively looked north up 7th Avenue as she pressed the button on the hand-held receiver, hit the horn twice, and turned the ignition key with the other hand.

"17 Adam to Central. Received Carnegie Hall at 57th and 7th. Fifteen blocks out, south of scene at 42nd and 7th. 17 Adam responding."

Seconds later, with her partner in tow, Officer Nicky Walsh gunned the cruiser up 7th Avenue through the rush hour traffic with lights flashing and sirens blaring.

Patrol cops responding to a crime scene are known as First Officers and have two major responsibilities, first to verify what the crime is, and second, to secure the scene.

For Nicky Walsh and her partner, the first question was easy. They had a homicide and, though the logistics of securing the crime scene were not easy, the presence of a retired cop left the scene uncompromised. By the time Patrol Supervisor Jim Connors arrived, they were ready.

Connors immediately called for six more patrol cars to help secure the scene and directed his First Officers to cordon off the entire block from 56th to 57th, surrounding Carnegie Hall with yellow CRIME SCENE DO NOT CROSS tape. He then positioned Officer Walsh at the front entrance while her partner detained the only two witnesses in the security office. Connors then instructed his partner to open a log and set up a temporary headquarters in the main lobby. The log would eventually contain a chronological list of every NYPD unit's response to the scene. Any person who entered the crime scene, along with a detailed list of any item recovered from the victim or the crime scene would be logged in.

Next, he called the medical examiner's office. Once the detectives finished their initial investigation and photography, the M.E. would be responsible for removal of the body. He knew FDNY paramedics had arrived simultaneously with the patrol officers and were with the victim. They had already made an official pronouncement of death, according to Officer Walsh. After notifying the Midtown North desk officer, who would pass on the information to higher-ups who were in a need to know position, Patrol Supervisor Connors put in a direct call to 18th Precinct Detective Supervisor, Lieutenant Tim Copeland.

* * *

The Midtown North Squad Commander was in his office early. He had no specific reason except to catch up on the overall operation of his detective squads. The Suits had been driving him crazy lately with public relations bullshit, and he was way behind on every case that had been opened or closed in the last week. Today's call would not help the situation. It had come from the Midtown North Patrol Supervisor.

"Copeland here."

"Good morning Lieutenant. This is Sergeant Conners at Carnegie Hall, and we have a world of shit coming down, sir."

"What have you got, Sarge?"

"Homicide, sir. You better get over here before the white shirts do. This is going to be big. Victim is Vincent Antonelli."

* * *

Detective Lieutenant Tim Copeland arrived at the entrance to Carnegie Hall in a foul mood. He wasn't mad at anyone, but he knew the call he received twenty minutes earlier meant a world of trouble for Midtown north and, especially, for him. As he stepped under the yellow tape that cordoned off the entire block around Carnegie Hall, he tried to take in the entire scene in one glance. He knew a lot had taken place before he arrived.

"Fill me in, Sarge," Copeland said, as Patrol Supervisor Jim Conners approached.

"Victim is Vincent Antonelli, conductor of the New York Philharmonic. He was scheduled to play here tomorrow night. It's been all over the media for a month. Paramedics already pronounced him. Stab wound to the neck. Seven patrol teams have the entire building secure, and emergency service just arrived to assist. Two witnesses being detained in a security office out back. Temporary headquarters is in the lobby, and the M. E. is on the way. And, just so you know, the press showed up about five minutes ago," Sergeant Connors replied.

"Yeah, I saw the Channel 4 truck when I got out. Everything else sounds by the book, Sarge. Crime Scene and Homicide should be here any minute. I want everyone kept out unless it is essential. This is going to be a cluster-fuck in every way possible. This concert was the biggest social event of the summer, and a lot of people are going to want answers fast. I don't want this scene compromised by rubbernecking white shirts and media. Do you understand, Sarge?"

"Yes, sir. How much leeway do I have to enforce that order?" Connors asked.

"You catch any shit, you direct it to me. I'll take the heat. Just keep them out."

As Sergeant Connors nodded and left to pass on the order, Tim Copeland turned to his detectives.

"Here's the deal. You guys work this case like it's the second coming of the Kennedy assassination until you hear different. No mistakes. Go over everything twice if you need to. Tie everything in with forensics and the M.E. You're to report everything back to me. I got a call to make."

Detective Squad Commander Tim Copeland stood in front of Carnegie Hall at 8:00 in the morning in the bright July sunshine and reached in his pocket for his cell phone. Normally, at this time of day, the crowds were thick and moving at a brisk pace up and down 57th Street. Today was no different, except the crowd had stopped and was watching the grand old music hall, from behind police lines, through flashing lights and mounting numbers of responding NYPD units.

* * *

Andy Wiley's morning started at 3:00 a.m. just like every other weekday. He got up, showered, shaved, dressed, grabbed a quick breakfast and headed for the station.

As usual, four hours later he was on location somewhere in the city, waiting to go on the air with a live feed concerning whatever story the bosses deemed newsworthy that particular day. Today he stood on 2nd Avenue, between 56th and 57th Streets, at the work site of another water line break, the fourth in the city this month.

Wiley had picked his spot. The camera was ready. Once again he checked his microphone and ear piece. With five minutes to spare, he waited for his cue.

A voice crackled in his ear.

"Wiley, this is Bailey. Drop what you are doing and get over to Carnegie Hall. The cops are crawling all over the place, and you are the closest mobile unit I have."

Andy Wiley was already moving. He put his hand over his mouth piece and yelled, "Shoot is off. Pack up everything as quickly as possible. We need to get our asses over to Carnegie Hall, like now."

Wiley walked to the van as the crew leapt into action. All the while he continued to talk into his microphone.

"Boss, did they say what was going on over there?"

"Nothing concrete, but sources tell us there could be a high profile homicide inside the Hall. Cops have the place cordoned off. Find out what you can and call back. Be ready to go to a live bulletin if we have to. Go! I want the jump on this," his boss replied.

Wiley pulled the seat belt across his chest as the van shot into traffic up 2nd Avenue and made a sharp left onto 56th Street.

"Already moving, boss. I'll be in touch."

* * *

The huge crowd would seem to be a godsend for a street musician, except for the fact they were all facing across the street. That was fine with the bearded, dread-locked saxophone player standing in the gathering crowd on 7th Avenue across from Carnegie Hall. This musician had no interest in playing the instrument he held, nor did he have the ability to play it. No one watching had more of an interest in the goings on, in and around Carnegie Hall, than the apparent struggling musician. Michael smiled knowingly when the white van with the red over-sized Number 4 emblazoned on its side screeched to a halt. He made a mental note of the handsome, dark-haired news reporter weaving his way through the thickening crowd toward the edge of the police barrier.

His main interest centered on the man standing out front talking on his phone. He smiled. He would follow this man's movements. For now, Tim Copeland would sit across the board from him.

* * *

Paul Worton could not get the image out of his head. He had seen it all in his twenty-five years on the force, especially the last fifteen as a New York City homicide detective. Every kind of degrading, violent act that could be done to the human body he had seen at one time or another. But the one thing that stuck in his mind no longer existed in reality. He did not think about it every waking hour, in fact, not even every day. But each time he left the on ramp to The Brooklyn Bridge crossing over to Manhattan, his eyes strayed to the place he did not want to look. Looking out over lower Manhattan, just as he did on another beautiful bright sunny morning, he could still see the smoke pouring out of the first Tower. Before his shock could register, he saw the second plane traveling too low and disappearing in a ball of flame into the Second Tower. The Towers were gone now, as were many friends and colleagues, but the image never faded, and he was sure it never would. The world changed for all Americans when The Twin Towers fell, but for the NYPD personnel who respond to crisis every day, September 11th left those who survived with feelings they were not prepared for. Helpless, grieving, unfounded feelings of guilt and tremendous loss. Those feelings multiplied daily, as the frantic search for survivors turned to the slow drudgery of endless recovery. As time passed, many stayed on the job, but many could not. Good men and women who just could not handle the constant reminder of fallen heroes and innocent victims left and moved away. A few turned to drugs and alcohol to forget. A few even took their own lives. For Worton, the empty space at the mouth of the Hudson always brought back the faces of friends and colleagues lost, on and long after, that bright sunny September morning.

Mercifully, the shrill ring of his cell phone interrupted his thoughts. Seeing Tim Copeland's name on the illuminated panel brought a frown to his face.

"This can't be good," he said, flipping the phone open.

"Worton here."

* * *

The disheveled musician sat on a folding chair next to an open leather case with his saxophone in his hand, quietly watching the action building across 7th Avenue. Michael let himself drift into a semi-state of meditation, slowly calming the adrenaline that had been building for twenty-four hours. Fifteen years in the making and his game for the ages had begun. His mind drifted back to the beginning.

As early as he could remember he sat across the table from his father learning the game. Jefferson Mueller loved the game of chess. His fascination with the game began while watching American Bobby Fischer destroy Russian Boris Spassky in the world chess championship during the summer of 1972. Soon after he joined a club and became a decent player, but what he wanted most was for his son to play with the greats of the world. Money was not an object. With his multi-million dollar inherited trust fund and a flourishing business as an art dealer, he could buy most anything he wanted. All Michael wanted was to please his father. He adored his father, and playing meant spending time together doing something they both loved. By the age of six, he was winning games against his father with ease. The older man enrolled his son in a private school and petitioned the best Grand Master in New York City, and president of The Manhattan Chess Club to tutor his son. For the next five years, the Master's teachings became the only important thing in the lives of both father and son. From teaching sessions, to practice games, to tournaments, they were inseparable. But though the young boy was very good and quite competitive in most tournaments, he never won. When he failed to get past the second round in The Greater New York Scholastic Chess Championships for the fifth straight time, The Master had seen enough. The boy would never forget the look on his father's face when The Master told him to take the boy home. The experiment was over.

Michael knew his father loved him, but the smashed dream changed their relationship forever. The boy was removed from private school and sent to public school where he excelled academically, but never fit in socially. Meanwhile, the boy's father immersed himself in his business and spent less and less time with Michael. The boy not only blamed himself for the lost relationship with his Dad, but for his Dad's depression and even, somehow, for his illness and subsequent death from prostate cancer. Long after the funeral and reception at their Sag Harbor home, he sat at his father's desk in the dark, silent study and vowed to make him proud.

Michael graduated first in his class and was accepted, early, to Harvard. By the time he finished four years at Harvard and two more at Rutgers School of Medicine, his plan was complete. When he turned twenty-one, at his mother's request, he took control of the family trust. She did not want to be bothered with the day-to-day business of managing the family money. As long as she was comfortable and active with her friends playing bridge twice a week, bowling on Wednesdays and bragging about her son the surgeon, she was content. But he was not a surgeon. He never did his residency in Chicago. Instead, he started his own training. He spent the next two years working with a summer stock theater group, starting out as a stage hand and working his way up through wardrobe, make-up and, finally, as an actor. During that time, he was a fanatic in the local gym putting on twenty-five pounds of muscle and bringing his body fat down to almost nothing. He left the theater, moved to Colorado and went to work as a ski instructor and personal trainer. His final two years, before coming home to New York, were spent working with a bounty hunter in California learning all he could about law enforcement and the use of various weapons. Coming full cycle, he moved back in with his mother in the small town of Sag Harbor. He told his mother he was a New York City surgeon. Meanwhile, Michael was finalizing his plan to challenge the New York City Police Department in his deadly game.

More sirens blared across the street and brought him out of his trance. The man he had been watching had been joined by a much younger blonde man. The disguised musician assumed the man must be a detective, but he was dressed differently than every other plainclothes police officer at the scene. The young officer wore sneakers, jeans and a sports coat. Both men stepped to the curb as an unmarked police car pulled up to the front entrance. A tall, dark-haired man in a suit got out and shook hands with the two men. He watched closely as the three men huddled together on the street corner. When they finished, the tall man from the car and the younger detective headed for the front entrance to Carnegie Hall. His first target pulled out his cell phone once again and began to talk.

The phony sax player picked up his case, folded his chair and started walking up 7th Avenue toward Central Park. He may have to rethink who his main adversary might be. The tall man intrigued him. There was something about the man. Something about the way he carried himself. The way he walked. Something.

Never mind Michael thought. Need to rest and plan. Game two starts early tomorrow.

* * *

Thirty minutes earlier, Detective 1st Grade Paul Worton flipped on the lights and siren in his car and banged a u-turn at the end of the bridge. The conversation with Tim Copeland had been very one-sided. He was being assigned to a high profile murder case at Carnegie Hall, and he was going on mandatory overtime. His leave and his weekend getaway with Lori were cancelled, and there was no telling when his life would be his again. The only thing Copeland left him was to call in his own guys. He called them first. The call to Lori would have to wait. He punched the button for Anthony's number and put the phone on speaker. Three rings later.

"Um, yeah Anthony, here," a groggy voice answered.

"Hey, Anthony," Worton yelled. "Wake up and get your sorry ass over to Carnegie Hall. We caught a big one and we don't have a choice. At least I don't and, if I don't, you don't. Some big wig over there has a spike sticking out of his neck and Copeland wants no screw-ups. I will be there in twenty minutes and you'd better be there first." He smiled as he hit delete and then punched Jose's number. Sometimes you just had to yell at Anthony to get him moving.

"Hello, Jose Morales speaking."

"Jose I need you, buddy. Copeland called me. I caught a beauty, and I'm going to need you," Worton said.

"What have you got?" Morales asked.

"You read about the big concert at Carnegie Hall tomorrow night? Antonelli and the Philharmonic are performing."

"Yeah. My wife is going with her mother and sister. Why?" Morales asked.

"Well, they won't see Antonelli. Someone tied him up and stuck him through the neck. He's dead and Copeland wants me, and I want you. How soon can you get there? Anthony is on his way and I will be there in twenty." Worton said.

"Well, I'm home, so it's going to take me at least an hour this time of day," Morales said.

"See you there. I gotta call Lori. We were supposed to go away for the weekend." Worton said.

"Good luck. I'm on my way." Morales said as he hung up.

Worton pressed the number one on his phone. After five rings Lori Worton's voice mail picked up.

"Hey Babe, bad news Copeland called and I have to go in. Vincent Antonelli has been murdered at Carnegie Hall, and he wants me to head up the investigation. You know how that goes. I don't have a choice. Sorry about the weekend. I will call you as soon as I can. Love ya," he said, as he maneuvered his car around a line of cars that had pulled over in deference to his siren. As he bolted past a taxi in Times Square, he wondered absentmindedly if the concert would go on without the conductor.

When he pulled up in front of Carnegie Hall, Lieutenant Copeland and Detective Anthony Austin were waiting for him.

The meeting with Tim Copeland was short and to the point. Worton would lead the investigation. All other departments of the NYPD would report their findings to Worton, and he would report to Copeland. Meanwhile, Worton's boss would run interference. He would keep the "White Shirts", all the way up to and including the mayor's office, off Worton's back. He would also deal with the media, answering all questions and being front and center for all press conferences.

Worton stood, arms folded, against the box seat door directly across from the lifeless body of famed conductor Vincent Antonelli. While his eyes never left the body, he was aware of the intricate ballet of investigators sifting around and through the crime scene. Every crime scene talks and crime scene detectives were busy taking photographs and collecting evidence. This could involve blood, fingerprints, weapons, or DNA - anything that could have been brought to the scene, or left at the scene, by the killer. The paramedics left after making the official pronouncement of death, and the medical examiner was standing by waiting to remove the body.

Detective Morales had arrived and was busy taking digital pictures. He knew that Worton would not want to wait for official pictures from Crime Scene. The only other Detective working the scene was Detective Austin.

Worton watched the young detective for a moment. Anthony stood in the middle of the marble staircase, staring first at the pool of blood on the stairs, then at the wall on the landing below. Over and over, Anthony's head moved back and forth, pausing for a second on the blood, and then on the wall.

"What have you got, Anthony?" Worton asked. Anthony looked up.

"Well, P.W., here's the deal. Someone ran down these stairs right through the blood and seems to have slammed into that wall at the bottom."

"Our Perp" Worton asked?

"Well, could be, but if 'it' is a 'he', then he has the smallest feet I have ever seen."

"And he was wearing high heels," Anthony said, smiling.

"Anthony, could we please keep the jokes to a minimum on this one? Are you telling me that a woman ran through this crime scene either during, or sometime after, the murder?" Worton asked.

"Exactly," Anthony said.

A forensic expert, dusting the banister for prints, spoke up. "Hey, lieutenant, I have a clear set of prints here. Entire hand, it looks like. It works with Anthony's footprints. This is a very small hand print."

"Thanks, Freddy," Worton said. "Jose, Anthony, come on up here for a minute." Soon the three detectives stood at the top of the stairs facing the dead man.

"What have we got so far?" Worton asked.

Detective Morales flipped open a small worn notebook and spoke.

"Ok. We think he was drugged down there in box thirty-three. Not sure how or with what. Just an assumption so far, but it seems he was taped to the chair and dragged to this spot. We found indent tracks still visible in the rug. Then, he was taped to the banister and killed."

"Not sure where the footprints and fingerprints fit in? That guy weighs a ton. No one that small dragged that body. Maybe more than one perp?" Anthony said.

Worton stared at the body. His mind was working quickly, and a sick feeling was building in his stomach.

"I hope I'm wrong boys, but I have a very bad feeling about this. Why not just kill him in the room? Why drag him out here? Not only a big name but on display for all to see. He wants to get someone's attention," he said.

Worton kept staring at the dead man. "Why do I think it's us he's trying to impress?"

* * *

GAME 2

July 13th

*"The essential quality of a high level player is a kind of enjoyment
of a very intense, physically and mentally exhausting struggle."*

Shelby Lyman

J orge Gonzales walked west on 25th Street to Broadway, then turned left heading down Broadway towards the Farmers' Market. The distinct smells of New York City change depending on time of year, time of day and the section of the city you are in. Upper East Side, Central Park, Midtown, Wall Street, Chinatown or Battery Park: every place different, yet totally part of the city. Jorge breathed deep, taking in the air of the early morning summer breeze. Sunshine, already bright, glistened off poles and roofs of the wide variety of tents and booths wrapped around the north end of Union Square, spilling out to encompass parts of the neighboring side streets.

Jorge purchased an orange and a corn muffin, as he weaved his way from vendor to vendor, enjoying the diversity of language and culture that permeated the crowds already gathered in the early morning sunshine. Patrons ranged from tourists, getting an early jump on the crowds, to local family food shoppers, to daily regulars picking up breakfast and hurrying on to eight or more hours as part of the city's enormous work force.

From the Farmers' Market on 14th Street, Union Square splits around a large common area surrounded by wrought iron fencing and dominated in the middle by a massive wooden flag pole topped by the Stars and Stripes. The great beauty of New York City lies in its diversity, for along with the taxis, trains, skyscrapers, restaurants and millions of people hurrying from place to place, you find a huge farmers' market in the middle of the street, and a beautiful serene park where people come to sit and read, to jog, walk or simply lie in the grass and nap.

Jorge entered the common, passing a statue of Abraham Lincoln and the cement base of the flagpole, as he made his way toward a mounted statue of George Washington at the opposite end of the park.

Jorge Gonzales made this trip every weekday morning before work. He was a self-made man, intensely proud of his Spanish/American heritage, born of dirt poor, but hard working, Puerto Rican parents in the poorest section of Spanish Harlem. His parents pushed him to stay in school and off the streets. At fifteen, he started working in the rail yards. Now, he was head of the union for the Long Island Railroad. Jorge was the first of his heritage to hold such a position. He was a proud man. Proud of his parents, his wife and children, his country, his heritage and the men and women he represented every day.

Jorge placed the orange and muffin on the base of Washington's monument and walked a few paces to the plaque situated in the middle of the wide cobblestone semi-circle at the front entrance to the square. The plaque inspired him to represent his people to the best of his ability, and he stopped to read it every day before getting his coffee.

UNION SQUARE PARK
Has been designated a
National Historical Landmark
Here workers exercised their right to
free speech and assembly and on Sept. 5th, 1882
Observed the 1st Labor Day

Jorge smiled to himself as he made his way to the Java Wagon. Those words always made him realize how important his job could be to so many people. He would enjoy breakfast and head for the office with a bounce in his step as usual.

The young businessman walked towards the mounted statue of Washington. Like almost everyone else in the plaza, Michael drank his coffee on the move while reading a folded section of newspaper with the long strap of his leather briefcase thrown over his shoulder. He looked like a young Wall Street businessman, wearing a gray business suit and sporting light blonde hair and a fashionable goatee. He slowed as he approached the front of the statue, seemingly intent on something in the paper that made him stop for a moment. No one paid any attention to him and, if they had, they could not have seen his hand slip from the folds of the paper or the syringe he held. The man slid the needle into the corn muffin and emptied the vial of cyanide in less than a second. He then turned the page on his paper, enveloping the syringe in one motion while moving to the right side of the statue.

Jorge Gonzales retraced his steps with a large cup of black Puerto Rican Bustello coffee, planning to enjoy what would be his last breakfast. Jorge took a sip of the steaming coffee and pulled the paper cupcake wrapping from his muffin. Taking a large bite, he watched the throngs of people streaming in every direction. He loved to watch people. Every morning was a melting pot of the world, in his opinion. Who were they? Where were they going? What did they do for a living, and what was their future?

He was halfway through the muffin before he realized something was wrong. He could not breathe. He could not talk.

He grabbed his throat and then grabbed the arm of the closest person to him. The woman screamed and tried to pry loose from the hand clutching her windbreaker. She was a tourist with her family, pushing one of her children in a stroller, and her husband quickly pushed Jorge away. He fell into the arms of another man who had been sitting next to him reading his paper.

The young man feigned surprise, then pretended to help the distressed man. Michael slipped a small folded paper into the breast pocket of Jorge's suit coat as he eased Gonzales to the ground. As Jorge's body convulsed, Michael stood and slowly melted back into the gathering crowd. Shouts were coming from different people.

"Someone, do something. "

"Call 911."

"Does anyone know CPR?"

The young man let the crowd press past him and then turned, walking slowly out of Union Square. He moved uptown towards Gramercy Park. Before Michael reached 14th Street, Jorge Gonzales died on the plaza where he came each day to make himself feel more alive.

* * *

Lori Worton flicked the switch to the lights and overhead fan just inside the door. The mixture of fragrance from candles, incense and potpourri wafted over her like an exotic perfume. She weaved through the display shelves and decorative arrangements until she reached the back room. Glancing at the antique grandfather clock, she realized she only had thirty minutes to ready the store for the morning crowd. Lori owned the store but rarely opened, preferring to cash out and close, rather than wake up at five and catch the early morning train, but Paul didn't have to be back to work until Monday and, for once, they had made plans for the weekend.

Lori smiled as she stuffed her purse under the counter. It would be nice to get away with Paul for a few days. Between, the shop, their teenage daughter running in twenty different directions, and Paul's job, juggling time together seemed harder and harder to pull off.

As "cruise director," a term of endearment their friends labeled her with years ago, Lori planned the weekend. After checking everyone's schedules, she rented a four bedroom beach house on the waterfront in Montauk, made a shopping list and called each couple with directions and a list of what to bring. Food, drinks and good friends would be just what the doctor ordered for all of them. Beach, sun, golf and volleyball during the day and charades, cards, and Trivial Pursuit at night, topped off by sitting around singing songs with Jeff on his guitar and Paul on the harmonica. Lori could not wait.

Lori's cell phone beeped just as she finished opening the cash register. Seeing her husband's screen name brought a frown to her face.

Few women could handle the message that ruined their weekend getaway as well as Lori Worton could. She knew the job, and she knew her husband did not have a choice. Lori worked as a dispatcher for the NYPD for twelve years and figured she would retire on the job. That was until September 11, 2001. Lori considered herself a pretty tough lady. She was a part of every case Paul had worked over their twenty years together. She had seen every file and picture and never shied away. But 9/11 was different. She made the calls that sent them in and listened to friends and colleagues rush to help. In her headphones, she heard it all unfold - and then silence. Deafening silence, as call number after call number never answered back. Lori stayed on for six months. Every time she sent a message, it reminded her of those who never returned her call. She knew she had to walk away.

Lori needed a change and knew her favorite store in Soho was for sale. Sweet old Annie Watts wanted to retire but wanted to leave the store with someone she could trust to keep it the same quaint style she cultivated for most of fifty years. Lori and the seventy-five year old grandmother were kindred spirits when it came to the collectible merchandise found inside *SWEET ANNIE'S*. Annie was thrilled by Lori's interest, and the rest came down to a fair price and the Worton's finding the right financing.

As she pulled open the blinds and walked to open the front door to the store, Lori made her decision.

She would go with the others to Montauk for the weekend. Paul would want her to go and, besides, who would act as cruise director if she didn't show up?

* * *

Paul Worton stretched out his long legs and crossed his ankles on the edge of his desk, leaning back in the hard-backed swivel chair. The front of Paul Worton's desk abutted the fronts of both Jose Morales' and Anthony Austin's in a kind of bloated T-formation. The configuration allowed the three men to face each other while working a case. It also allowed for plenty of surface space to spread out the contents of an open file.

Every item tagged at the Antonelli crime scene or at the medical examiner's office had been photocopied. Those photocopies and digital photos from Morales' camera littered the combined steel gray metal desktops. The crime scene photos were in the right hand corner of Worton's desk. Photocopies of the contents of the victim's pockets and wallet were in the left hand corner. All canvas statements taken at or near the scene, including those of the security guard and the janitor, sat on Anthony's desk. Written reports from paramedics, the first patrol officers on the scene, and the patrol supervisor were in the middle of his desk. The autopsy report and all official crime scene photos would go on Morales' desk as soon as they came in.

Worton held a statement from the victim's chauffeur in his hand. It contained his first lead. Gunter Wilhelm arrived at the

Tom Blenk

back entrance to Carnegie Hall at 9:00 a.m. sharp. According to the police officer's report, he was not very cooperative at first, insisting he must be let through to pick up his boss. Did the officer not know who Vincent Antonelli was? He must not be kept waiting.

Worton smiled at the officer's reply that "Antonelli would be waiting for quite some time before his ride came, and then it would be by ambulance with no need of sirens." After some questioning, Wilhelm allowed that he had last seen his boss at 9:30 p.m. the previous evening, and been given instructions to wait by the back door and escort a young woman into the back entrance when she arrived. He was then to go home and not to return until precisely 9:00 a.m. the following morning unless Mr. Antonelli called with other instructions. He had done as instructed and had not heard from the conductor since.

The report was detailed, and held much more from Gunter Wilhelm on his duties for the great conductor, but Worton was interested in his description of the young woman who entered Carnegie Hall a little before midnight.

Asian descent, five-two or three, maybe a hundred pounds. Very beautiful, according to the German chauffeur, with alabaster white skin, almost porcelain in looks, with long, jet-black hair. She wore a black skirt, heels, shawl and a purple blouse. When asked if he knew what she was doing there, the chauffeur would only say she had business with Antonelli, and he was not privy to what that business might be.

Worton dropped the report on the desk as Morales banged through the squad room door.

"Find anything in there?" Morales asked, pointing at the desk as he weaved his way around various obstacles of people and objects to reach their private alcove in the back of the room.

"Just that we have to find the Asian girl and go back at this chauffeur again. He knows more than he is telling about Antonelli," Worton answered. "You get anything?"

"Yeah, seems this guy Antonelli has plenty of enemies, and I may have a lead on this Asian girl. Which do you want first?" Morales said, flopping into one of the chairs opposite Worton.

"Really? Let's hear about the girl first."

"Well, it seems in the world of concert violinists, there is an eighteen year old Chinese protégé who is renowned in Asia and Europe."

"Who knew?" Worton said, leaning back to listen.

"Her name is Kim Soo. She and her chaperone parents are here in the U. S. on a whirlwind tour and, the night before last, she had a private dinner with one Vincent Antonelli. Rumor mill has it he was about to offer her, and I am quoting here because I have no idea what it means, First Violin with the Philharmonic." Morales continued.

"First Violin in any orchestra is a big thing. In the New York Philharmonic it is arguably the pinnacle of the profession. She is awfully young for that distinction, no matter how good she might be," Worton mused.

"That brings me to Antonelli's enemies, and why he may have so many," Morales said, flipping through his notes. "Seems this is not so nice a guy. According to his contemporaries and the orchestra members we have found so far, he was a hugely talented asshole. He used the power of his position to manipulate every part of his life and everyone he had power over. He made career and financial promises to dozens of people that he never followed through on. And he had the power to brush them off when push came to shove. Seems he reveled in the fact that most people could not touch him."

"So, you are telling me that everyone hated the guy, and anyone he knew could be a suspect. What does that have to do with the young girl?" Worton asked.

"I'm getting to that. During his career with the Philharmonic, there have been rumors of sexual misconduct by Antonelli with female orchestra members. No charges were ever filed and no sanctions against him," Morales said, reading again from his notes. "As soon as they heard he was dead, they started talking. Three different, former, female members claim he traded entry into the orchestra for sexual favors. Two went along, and he kept his promise until he tired of them, then he gave them glowing references to other top orchestras. The third said no, and he kept his promise to her, also. She never played in a top band, and all her accusations fell on deaf ears." Morales looked up at Worton. "Seems our victim had a penchant for young talented girls he could bully."

"We don't have the prints back yet, but I don't believe in coincidence. A person with small hands and feet ran through that crime scene, and a hundred pound Asian girl was in the building around the time of this pervert's death. We need to find that girl, Jose." Worton said.

Detective Morales smiled.

"Just thought I would stop by to fill you in and pick up Anthony. They are staying at The Hilton on 7th Ave."

"Nice work. Anthony is at the training center. You know he can't start his day without his workout. From there, he is going straight to the M.E.'s office for the autopsy. Grab Mike Stellos downstairs on your way out. You know Mike. Homicide sent him over and he's with us for the duration. He went down to get a coffee. Tell him to drink on the run." Worton spoke without looking up. He was already reaching for the photocopies of Antonelli's belongings.

*　*　*

Kim Soo never raised her voice to her parents in her life. Never went against their wishes, never even used the word no in their presence. Now she had defied them. She could hear them arguing in the spacious living room of their four-room luxury suite. Her parents believed they were staying at the New York Hilton due to the kindness of Conductor Vincent Antonelli, and they were outraged that she would dare to speak of leaving without contacting him first. They did not know the real reason for his generosity, and she could not tell them where she had been and what she had seen. They argued all night. She told them she wanted to leave New York on the next flight. That she didn't want to play the violin any more. She wanted to go back home to China and live a quiet life. Her parents were confused and angry. Finally, they were stunned when she screamed at her father that they were leaving and that it was final.

Now as she sat on her bed next to her packed suitcase listening to her parent's heated conversation in the next room, images she would not soon forget pounded in her head.

* * *

Kim Soo arrived by taxi and walked the two blocks to Carnegie Hall. She moved quickly behind the main building to the back entrance where Vincent Antonelli's long-time chauffeur waited. He let her in and left for the night, per his instructions. It was not the first time he had closed his eyes to his boss's indiscretions.

Kim Soo moved through the corridors of the bottom floor of the Great Hall as if in a trance. With her head down, she slowly climbed the long marble stairs leading to the reserved boxes where she knew the great conductor awaited her arrival. Six steps from the top she stopped. A red trickle of liquid dripped from step five to step six. It seemed oddly out of place in the ornate main entryway. She skirted slowly around the small dark puddle, staring back at it as she reached the top step.

Her tormentor stared at her through dead, lifeless eyes. Kim Soo staggered for a second, bracing herself with her hand on the marble banister. She had never seen a dead person before, and her first thought was to scream for help. But no, she stifled that. It was obvious that no one could help Vincent Antonelli now, and her being at the scene could not help her situation. Panic set in next, and she bolted from the top step, almost falling head-first down the length of white marble stairs, slamming her shoulder into the landing wall as she turned the corner. In seconds she was running down 7th Avenue, wishing she were thousands of miles away, safe in bed, in her small hometown of Cinching, China.

* * *

Anthony listened with one ear to the drone of the M.E.'s voice as the technician moved from one end of the metal table to the other, talking into the thin microphone that curved around his chin to his lips. Anthony leaned against the door frame, chewing on his pen with his notepad dangling from the fingers of his right hand. He never got used to the cold clinical nature of the autopsy of a human being. To him, once the body came here, stripped and lying bare, it ceased to be human anymore. Even though he had seen every kind of death during his three years in homicide, the victim was still a person to him until he got here and heard the whir of the saw and watched the M.E. slice open the chest cavity. Rarely did he learn anything of interest at an autopsy, but Worton wanted someone here and, usually, he got the job. Everything the M.E. found would be sent to their office as soon as it could be processed. Everything from photos, to forensics, to all related paperwork, including the M.E.'s written report and findings, would be in the package.

Anthony smiled and shook his head. Could it really be only three years in homicide and eight years on the force? It seemed like twenty years since he enrolled in the Academy to try and get some direction in his life. At the age of twenty-one, after getting a degree in business from a small college in New Hampshire, he went to work as an assistant pro at a golf course next to the campus. He figured it would be a good place to start his career. Anthony went to New Hampshire for the skiing in the winter and the golf in the summer and the girls all year long. It all seemed to be working fine until he decided to join a couple of buddies on a trip to Vegas the winter after graduation.

The second night in town, he and Joey left the other two at the blackjack table and headed out to find a strip club. Anthony's next memory was waking up in a strange bed, naked, with a massive six foot five gorilla telling him to get dressed and get out of his apartment. On the taxi ride back to the hotel, images started to return of a perfect female body on stage and then in his lap—a hazy image of a wild, half-naked taxi ride to a small, brightly lit house with flowers and rows of chairs and a guy on a stage that looked like Elvis. It came back to him in a rush, the "I do's," the fake reception, more booze and a night of wild sex. He remembered her name was Vicky, and her body was perfect, and he had married her.

His buddies were at the hotel, and they were about to call the cops when he walked in. Joey told how he went to take a leak when Vicky was giving him a lap dance and, when he returned, they were both gone.

After explaining that he was probably married, and after listening to their abuse for awhile, they set out to find Vicky, his stripper wife.

Two weeks later, his buddies were back in New Hampshire telling his bizarre story while he was living in California with Vicky the stripper and her six-year old daughter. He had flown home to tell the family of his new-found status, and they had not reacted well. In fact, they pretty much disowned him. Once in California, they discovered the Vegas wedding was not legal. So, on Super Bowl Sunday, in Vicky's backyard, they got remarried, had a cookout and then watched the game. At first it seemed the perfect life. He got up late each day and headed for the golf course. At night he would baby sit his new best buddy, and have unbelievable sex when the wife got home from dancing naked in front of a hundred guys. The fun lasted about three months.

One day Anthony woke up and didn't want to play golf. He also didn't want to be married or have a child. He wanted to go home. He soon learned that his new wife was not only possessive, but even a bit of a stalker. It took a year of legal action, money, and restraining orders to make the divorce final, and almost as long to mend fences with his parents. What drove him to search for a new start away from New Hampshire and, eventually, to the Police Academy, was the constant ribbing and embarrassment garnered by the telling and re-telling of his Vegas adventure. Eight years later, at the ripe old age of twenty-nine, those same critics were still amazed by his career choice.

Anthony straightened up from his slumped position against the door jam as the harsh sound of the saw broke into his daydream. His last thought of the two year ordeal was of Vicky. Man! She was crazy but boy, what a body, he thought, smiling and shaking his head.

* * *

Detective Jose Morales realized the moment the door opened to Suite Five Sixty One that this would be one tough interview. The very distinguished Chinese gentleman who answered the door spoke little English, and it was quite a few moments before they were allowed to enter the room. While still in the hallway, he called dispatch to get a translator ASAP. The Asian couple sat together on a purple satin ottoman. The woman was obviously scared and chattered loudly at her husband until the man held up his hand. It was not a request; it was an order, and she lowered her head and was instantly quiet.

"We are Chinese. We visit. We do nothing wrong. Why police here?"

He tried to put up a strong front, but Morales had been doing this a long time, and he recognized fear when he heard it. He decided to get right to the heart of the matter.

"Sir, as I said in the hallway, we are New York City police detectives, and we are here to talk to your daughter. Could you please tell her we are here?" Morales said.

"No! She not here. She go home last night,"

"Sir, I do not want to scare you, but you need to understand. I will put a man outside your door and wait to get a court order, and then we will search your room. I know you want to protect her, but I need to talk to her and I think she is here." Morales said quietly.

"No! She no trouble. She play violin. You not need talk her," the man pleaded.

Before Detective Morales could speak, a door to his right opened and Kim Soo entered the room. He was struck by her beauty and how vulnerable she looked. Her father's voice stopped her in her tracks. He stood lecturing her in Chinese, the octave rising with each word. Her answer was swift and sharp, and the only word Morales understood was "Antonelli." Whatever she said had a dramatic effect on both parents. Her mother wailed and put her head in her hands while her father sat back down with a stunned look on his face. Kim Soo sat in a chair opposite the detectives, folded her hands in her lap, and waited.

"How may I help you?" She asked, in what detective Morales was happy to note was very good English.

"I am Detective Morales and this is my partner Detective Stellos. We are here to investigate the murder of Vincent Antonelli. We found fingerprints at the scene. When we put our info in the computer, your name came up on our international database," Morales said. "We know you were there last night. We need to know when and why."

Kim Soo spoke clearly and quietly for close to an hour. She told the truth and answered every question the detectives asked. By the time she was done, she was no longer a suspect in Jose Morales's eyes, and she was no longer their innocent little girl in her parents' eyes.

When Detective Morales left the room, he felt sorry for Kim Soo. It would be a long time before she could explain her actions to her parents, and she would have to stay in town for the time being. More importantly, they would probably be able to eliminate Kim Soo as a suspect soon. Morales had been on the job a long time and usually knew when a suspect was lying to him. This girl was too scared to lie, but at least they came away with a partial time line for the crime.

They headed back to The House. Worton would be waiting.

* * *

The American Academy of Dramatic Arts is located at 120 Madison Avenue. The school opened in 1884, but the present day location wasn't built until 1907. The white, six-story building houses three theaters, classrooms, rehearsal halls, dance studios, dressing rooms, a prop department, production workshops, a costume department, a library, and a student lounge. The prestige of the Academy is unquestioned, having produced 72 Oscars, 205 Emmys, and 58 Tony nominations over more than a century. Lauren Bacall and Ann Bancroft, Judd Hirsch and Kate Jackson, Elizabeth Montgomery and Frank Morgan, Robert Redford and Don Rickles, to name just a few, have entered the classrooms and graced the stages of The American Academy of Dramatic Arts. But, in the end, the Academy is a school like any other school and, for more than fifty years, Professor Clifton Davenport has been the school's administrative and academic icon.

Professor Davenport came to the Academy as a sixteen year old high school sophomore seeking a part-time job. He started out sweeping the floors and taking out the trash after school for seventy-five cents a week. Every day, from the beginning, he paid attention to everything that happened at the Academy. As years passed, he became a fixture, helping backstage with lighting and sets during productions, and working his way into most classrooms, sitting in back rows and taking in all he could learn. The professor never aspired to be an actor. His first love was the Academy itself and its ability to turn raw talent into the stars of stage and screen. Through high school and four years at NYU business school, Cliff Davenport continued to work at the Academy, doing anything and everything asked of him, making himself invaluable to administrators and teachers alike.

After graduation, an administrative assistant job was waiting. For the next ten years he worked his way up to Associate Director of Admissions, all the while taking courses to acquire his B.A. in theater in an effort to learn all he could about every department in the school. Now, fifty years later, he was just starting his fifth year as President of the Academy of Dramatic Arts.

Cliff Davenport never taught a class at the Academy, but over the years the title of "Professor" seemed to evolve as part of his name with both teachers and students. "The Professor" loved the title and prided himself in knowing all there was to know about his school and all of his students.

What he did not know as he unlocked the front door to the Academy on a bright sunlit July morning was that he was being watched, and that he only had three days to live.

* * *

The young street merchant set up shop across from The Midtown North Police Station. Michael knelt at the curb and opened the faded box style suitcase. First, he removed ten aerosol paint cans of various colors and lined them evenly on the curb. Next, four cardboard ovals, two putty knives and a copy of The New York Times were placed within an arm's reach. The man wore a t-shirt, paint splattered jeans and an old pair of sneakers. He had a mustache, a five o'clock shadow, and his sun-bleached shoulder length hair was pulled back in a pony tail. He unzipped a black portfolio briefcase and began to set several 16" x 20" paintings on small wooden stands facing the pedestrian side of the curb.

The artist immediately went to work. He knelt on a towel at the curb and placed a sheet of cardboard in front of him. His hands flashed as he moved from one aerosol can to another. Using a combination of crumpled newspaper, various cardboard circles and the two different sized putty knives, he turned the blank canvas into a mystical painting of Times Square. Fifteen minutes later, when he placed the finished product on the sidewalk with the other New York landscapes, a fascinated crowd had gathered. He would stay busy and make some money at twenty bucks per painting all in the name of waiting to get a second look at his opponent. Michael's peripheral vision never left the front entrance of the 18th Precinct.

* * *

The door to Lieutenant Tim Copeland's office would have been better suited as a revolving door rather than one with a doorknob. Men in suits and men in uniform continued to follow one another in and out of the office at regular intervals. As they came and went, they glanced to the back of the room where the three detectives were huddled. They all wanted answers in connection with the Carnegie Hall murder and Detective Paul Worton knew Copeland was running interference for him. The squad room itself was crowded with police officers and civilians, some working the Antonelli case while others were not. The noise was loud and constant, and beginning to bother Worton's concentration.

The angle of Paul Worton's chair was so severe that it seemed it had to tip over, but he knew how to work the tilt of the worn wooden swivel chair as well as he knew how to work the stick shift of the vintage BMW sitting in his garage at home. He teetered there with his heels just barely on the desk and his arms dangling over each side of the chair. For the time being, the papers he held in each hand were forgotten. He listened carefully to Anthony's voice, but kept his eyes on the office across the room.

Detective Anthony Austin may have been bored at the autopsy, but he was thorough about every detail of his job and that included giving a report. He was meticulous and that was why Worton liked working with him, but today his notes revealed little if anything they did not already know.

"OK. Anthony. Good job. Not much there. Did they say when we might get the forensic results?" Worton asked.

"Couple of days they hope. They said it would be an A-1 priority." Anthony answered.

"Right. What we do have is our photos from the scene, interviews with orchestra members, the chauffeur's story, canvas interviews, interviews with Antonelli's friends and relatives, photocopies of everything from the scene and the autopsy, Jose's interview with the Chinese family and photocopies of everything found on Antonelli's person and wallet." Worton said, reading from a checklist in his hand.

"Anything of interest on him?" Morales asked.

"No, the usual stuff: keys, handkerchief, tin of Altoids and the wallet. Actually, it's a billfold. Regular stuff there too: cash, credit cards, business cards – one of his and a couple of others. He had a note from someone about some musical piece and a piece of paper with some kind of chart on it. I couldn't figure that one out. Maybe you'll have better luck." Worton said, handing one of the papers to Detective Morales.

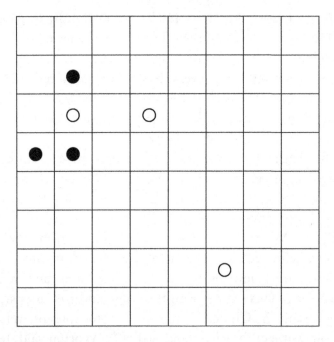

Morales studied the paper for a moment and then handed it to Anthony.

"Beats me, some sort of graph or game? How about musical notes? I don't know much about music, but he certainly did." Morales said. Anthony glanced at it and handed it back to Worton.

"Maybe it's a map or code, why? You think it means something?" Anthony asked.

Worton pushed away from the desk and stood up rifling papers together into a stack.

"I doubt it, but I know we need to piece together what we do know and I can't concentrate here. Let's grab the file and head for O'Mally's. I'm starved and we can get some quiet there in the back of the room. You guys get the car. I'll run this by Copeland and let him know where we will be."

The three men gathered everything from the desks and headed for the door.

The King's Gambit

* * *

Twenty minutes later, Paul Worton was the last to enter O' Mally's Bar. Something made him hesitate at the door. He held it open for a moment, looked left and then right down the length of 33rd Street between 5th Avenue and Broadway. He had a sudden premonition that he was being watched. It was just a feeling. He had seen nothing out of the ordinary on the busy New York side street but something made him look and that bothered him. He shook his head and entered the bar.

O'Mally's is a watering hole for detectives all over the city. Most New York City police detectives work four day tours, with two back to back nine hour shifts, followed by two eight hour shifts. The nine hour shifts run from 4:00 p.m. to 1:00 a.m. while the two eight hour shifts run from 8:00 a.m. until 4:00 p.m. Three of the four shifts allow a fifteen or sixteen hour turnaround, giving cops time to commute, get a home cooked meal, spend time with the family and try to live a normal life for awhile. The "turn around shift" is different. This swing shift, between the end of the one a.m. shift and the start of the eight a.m. shift, only leaves a seven hour window, and for most cops the commute home could be as much as two hours one way. Veterans call it "swinging out" and everyone has a different way to spend the off hours when going home just makes no sense. Some hang out at the precinct and play cards or watch TV. Others get a quick bite to eat and then get some much needed sleep in the duty room. Some workaholics stay at their desks drinking coffee and catching up on paperwork. The rest go out with their buddies to places like O'Mally's for a drink, some good food and to share stories of another day on the job.

Like many bars and restaurants in the city, O'Mally's main seating area is in the back rather than the front. A massive dark mahogany bar encompassed the right hand wall just inside the entrance. Half of the fifteen matching bar stools were occupied as Worton and his team entered. The walkway between the stools and a line of two person tables on the left was narrow enough that most patrons turned hips side-to-side as they moved from the front to the back of the bar. The place was littered with cops from Upper Manhattan to Battery Park. It had been a rough week all over the City.

Worton and his crew shook a few hands and acknowledged others as they weaved their way past the white tablecloths and made their way to the back room. The room was dimly lit but quite spacious. Several of the large booths lining the walls were occupied, and four couples sat at two of the ten dinner tables in the center of the room.

A large round black oak table situated in the back corner of the room was perfect for their needs, and it was empty. It was surrounded by a padded bench seat, seating eight people comfortably and had all the surface area they would need to lay out their paperwork. The plan was to order food and drinks, and then read every report and look over every photo individually before any discussion took place. Phase two would be to discuss everything they had, piece by piece, and, finally, try to figure out where to go from here.

* * *

Paul Worton sipped his Captain Morgan and Diet Pepsi as he surveyed each item from the file before passing it to his left. The appetizers arrived quickly. Anthony, Jose Morales and Mike Stellos had a pitcher of beer going but, bottom line, this was not a social event. They needed a game plan, a direction, a suspect. The heat was already coming down.

An hour later, they were halfway through discussing the file when Worton's right arm went numb as a hand clamped down on the soft tissue between his neck and shoulder. He winced as the fingers locked momentarily in the famous "Spock" hold. Worton jerked free and whirled to confront the smiling face of his assailant.

"Worton you dog! What the hell are you doing here? Working on the overthrow of Midtown North?" the voice of Detective Sam Jameson boomed.

Worton's pain and anger quickly faded into a huge grin.

The big man always commanded attention. His loud voice and six-foot-five, two hundred sixty pound frame, coupled with an infectious grin, made him hard to ignore. Worton always felt better after an encounter with Sam.

Sam Jameson and Paul Worton hit it off from the day they met at the Police Academy. They entered the Academy oblivious to each other's existence and graduated six months later as best friends. Outside the job, their families became close and they socialized together whenever their schedules allowed, which wasn't often enough for anyone. Their careers mirrored each other, from rookie patrol, to detective, to homicide, but Worton worked out of Midtown North while Jameson patrolled the other end of the city in Manhattan South, making their chance encounters on the job pretty rare.

Worton grabbed his friend in a hug that barely got his arms around the big man's shoulders.

"Haven't you heard we are planning your retirement party? The bosses want you out."

"Good, they can't want me out as bad as I want out. All they have to do is double my pension and I am gone." Jameson laughed.

"Are you kidding? You should be paying them you tight-wad. You still have the first dime you ever earned," Worton shot back. "Tell me is Emma still alternating the two dresses she owned when you guys got married? Or did you break down and buy a new one for the tenth anniversary?"

"Hell no! But I did take her to the Salvation Army the other day to get some shoes. Figured it doubled as a night out." Jameson dead panned.

Worton turned back to the table.

"Sit down a minute Sam. You know my squad except maybe Mike Stellos here. He's down from Homicide working a case with us."

Jameson shook hands with everyone and slid in the booth next to Worton.

"Nice to meet you Mike. My condolences on working with these misfits. Jose, how's the family? And you, Anthony, any side trips to Vegas lately to see the ex? You know it's much harder to get suckered into a quickie wedding these days now that the Elvis Chapel is closed."

Jose grinned and Anthony shook his head.

"You need new material Sam. It's the same line every time." Anthony said.

"I know. But I don't have time to write new stuff. Every time I try, they make me solve a murder. What is up with that?" He laughed. "Hey, I heard you guys caught a big one. The Carnegie Hall deal? Man I wouldn't want that, too many white shirts breathing down your neck."

Sam grabbed a glass as he talked and poured himself a beer.

"Got a nut twister myself though. Head of the LIR union got whacked in Union Square the other day. Everybody thought it was a heart attack but turns out he was poisoned. The autopsy showed cyanide. Just got back from a full day of trying to piece it together. I thought I would drop by for a bite to eat before heading back to the barn. Boys should be back with witness statements by then."

"Yeah, we got the scumbag conductor that nobody liked except the people that didn't know him. The station is like the freeway at rush hour with people who want answers now," Worton sighed. "We needed to get away from there to sort out what we have and where we go from here. We were just going over the file and bouncing things off each other".

As Paul Worton talked, Detective Jameson absently sifted through the pile of photographs on the table.

"Maybe we can get some of that Manhattan South expertise." Anthony joked.

But Worton was watching his friend. It was one of the few times since they met that the big man was not smiling. Sam Jameson was staring at the last picture he had picked up.

"What is this Paul?" He asked, handing the photo to Worton.

The picture showed the white piece of paper found in Vincent Antonelli's billfold.

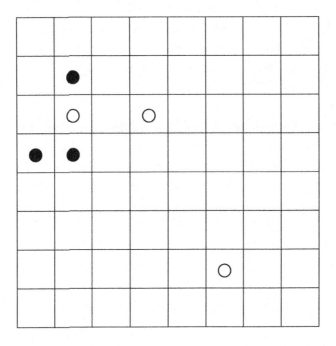

"Crime scene photo from the victim's belongings. Stuff from his billfold. Why?" Worton wanted to know.

Detective Jameson was all business now.

"Folded into a small square?" He asked.

"Yeah Sammy. Why?"

"Cause' my vic had a white folded piece of paper that looked a lot like this in the breast pocket of his sports coat." Jameson said.

"This one was folded inside a pocket of my guy's billfold. You sure they are the same?" Worton asked as he eased closer to his friend.

"Well the paper and lines look the same but there are only two circles on mine. One white and one black. One at the top and one at the bottom of the page." Jameson answered.

Morales whistled and took the photo from Worton.

"Think there is a connection Paul?" He said.

"Maybe he was into music too," Anthony added. "If you were right about it being musical notes or something like that."

"I don't know. But you better call your boss, Sam. I'm calling Copeland now." Worton said, as Morales dropped the photo on the table.

He got up and stepped out a back door into the ally. All his happiness at seeing Sam was suddenly replaced by the same bad feelings he had at Carnegie Hall three nights earlier.

He hoped he was wrong but his gut told him they were not just musical notes in the photo, and he did not believe in coincidence. He believed both folded notes were left where they were so they would be found. The question was by who? And why?

* * *

Andy Wiley sat staring at his computer screen shaking his head. It was hard to comprehend that he had gone from a guy on a street corner with a monotonous two minute water break story to a national news personality in the space of three days. Not only was he the first to tell New York's early risers about the famous conductor's death, but his feed found its way to Matt Lauer on the Today Show, and Diane Sawyer on Good Morning America.

"Unbelievable," he whispered, shaking his head. "I have to watch it one more time."

Wiley moved the cursor and clicked the Real Time Player icon on the flat screen. Channel 4's local morning show, featuring the daily traffic report was in full swing. New York traffic grids suddenly gave way to a white screen with the word, *BULLETIN*, emblazoned in red. This screen quickly gave way to the news desk and Channel 4's early morning anchor, Karen Meadows, who was all business as she spoke.

"We have breaking news of a possible homicide at Carnegie Hall and we will now go to our correspondent, Andy Wiley, at the scene."

"Andy?"

The picture showed bright morning sunshine beating down on a growing crowd held back by police officers and yellow crime scene tape. Andy Wiley stood with the Great Hall in the background and waited for the red light on the camera to go to green and the prompt from Karen Meadows.

"Karen, sources here at Carnegie Hall tell us that Vincent Antonelli, renowned conductor of The New York Philharmonic, was murdered here last night. We believe Mr. Antonelli was stabbed to death somewhere between 11:00 p.m. and one in the morning."

Karen Meadows stared intently at her monitor trying to look as serious as possible.

"Andy, do we know why Mr. Antonelli might have been there last night?" She asked.

"Well, Karen, for those who were not aware, Mr. Antonelli had arranged for The Philharmonic to return to its original home here at Carnegie Hall after a forty-four year absence. The concert was scheduled for tomorrow night and was the most anticipated symphony event of the season. It is assumed, at this point, that he was here in some connection to the concert." Andy replied.

Again the screen shifted back to the station.

"Do we know if the concert will go on as planned, Andy?" Karen Meadows asked.

"No, Karen, we have had no comment from Carnegie Hall officials or members of the Philharmonic," Andy answered.

Back at the studio Karen spoke again.

"What else can you tell us about the crime itself?"

"We know there was only one victim, and it is very early in the investigation, so no suspects. We do know it was a stabbing and a murder weapon was found, although we have not been told just what was used to kill Mr Antonelli. I am going to try to speak directly to the detective in charge." Andy said.

"OK, Andy, thank you. We will be waiting to hear what you can learn." Karen replied.

"This is Andy Wiley, live, in front of Carnegie Hall the show place of so many brilliant performances, but today, the stage for a horrible tragedy."

As the screen went blank, Andy Wiley leaned back in his chair grinning from ear to ear. It was good. Real good. And he was reaping the benefits. Bailey gave him the story to run with, and hinted toward the possibility of filling in as a weekend anchor. But Wiley would weigh his options. He already had an option from *The Daily News* for a byline about the Antonelli murder, and a possible weekly column. He was well aware of how the news business worked and this one moment in the spotlight could send his career soaring.

Something caught his eye. Something in the bottom left hand corner of the screen. Two small words were blinking on and off. **"click here" "click here"**

The words were smaller than anything he had seen on his computer before and flashed in a different color each time they reappeared.

Wiley slid the cursor down to the message.

He hesitated for a moment, not really knowing why. He double clicked on his mouse.

A close up of Vincent Antonelli's lifeless body leaped from the screen to his eyes. The dead man was tied to a chair, with some sort of sharp object, with a handle, impaled in his neck. Bright red blood was everywhere and Adam Wiley could hardly breathe. It took a few seconds before he realized there were words printed at the top of the screen.

DOES THIS HELP YOUR STORY
WOULD YOU LIKE TO KNOW MORE
YES   NO
CLICK ON ONE

A moment later Adam Wiley clicked *YES*.

* * *

GAME 3
July 16th

"Chess is the ability to use every quality you have, every attribute and every character trait in the struggle against another person."
Shelby Lyman

It was a homicide Detective's worst nightmare. A serial killer with no obvious motive and no suspect in sight. The two similar clues from murders in opposite ends of the city now stood at three. The call to Tim Copeland from O'Mally's set a city wide alert in motion. The word went out. Every death anywhere in or around the city would be on the lookout for a small folded piece of paper with squares and dots on it. Two days later the detective's hunch became fact.

As a teacher, Jennifer Mathewson went to work on the morning of July sixteenth with her daily goal in mind: maybe today she would find the next Bogart or the next Hepburn. Instead, she found Professor Cliff Davenport hanging from the archway in the main foyer of The American Academy of Dramatic Arts.

The crime scene was only fifteen minutes old when the investigation team did a cursory search of the victim looking for one particular item. They found the white paper tucked in the professor's shirt pocket. It took a second to sink in before they halted all activity and called the Task Force that the Manhattan Chief of Detective's Office had set up twenty four hours earlier.

Paul Worton stood in a corner near the door to the conference room. The room was set up as a temporary hub for the newly formed Task Force. The bosses from Midtown North and Manhattan South, with approval from the Police Commissioner's Office, chose Worton's boss, Tim Copeland, to lead the team. He had every division within the NYPD from patrol on up, including Major Case, Criminal Assessment and Criminal Profiling, at his disposal, and they were all hard at work before Worton's eyes. Copeland chose Worton to be his point man on the investigation. The first Task Force meeting of all parties involved would take place at 10:00 p.m. Everything collected from all three crime scenes, every interview, every report and every piece of evidence, would be evaluated at that time. They needed a direction and so far they had nothing.

Directly in front of him, every officer who had responded to each of the three crime scenes was being interviewed by Major Case detectives. They would go over every detail of their written reports. Over their heads, along the far wall, prints of the three separate pieces of paper found on each victim were blown up and hanging side by side.

Every few minutes, Worton looked up and stared at the photos. What did they mean? Who or what did they represent? The killer left them and he left them to send a message. Experts were pouring over the originals looking for some clue to their meaning. The killer was talking to them but they had yet to decipher the language.

Officers Scotty Ryan and Nicky Walsh stepped into the room to meet with investigators about the Carnegie Hall murder. The barrel-chested veteran walked right in and started greeting every cop in the room that he knew, which turned out to be just about everyone.

Nicky Walsh hung back and took it all in. This is where she wanted to be some day: in the middle of a major crime investigation, preferably as a homicide detective. Nicky's eyes scanned the room flickering over each activity until they reached the overblown photos on the wall. She tilted her head, squinted and took a small step towards them. She frowned and glanced away for a second, as if looking for someone or something, then turned back to the photos.

Paul Worton could not help watching her as she stepped directly in front of him. Her reaction to the photos intrigued him. He spoke to the young officer.

"What do you see officer?"

Nicky Walsh was startled. She did not see him standing in the corner behind her.

"Sorry. Didn't see you there," she said, moving to the side.

"No problem. I'm Detective Paul Worton. I'm kind of in charge here, but they do all the work so I stay out of the way." He said, with a smile.

"Sorry, Sir I didn't recognize you at first. I know who you are. I am Officer Nicky Walsh. I think my dad knew you." She said.

Worton was taken aback for a moment. He recognized her dad's blue flashing eyes and her mom's dark, almost olive, skin.

"No need to be sorry Officer, and please don't call me sir. It's Paul," he said, offering his hand. "You're Nicolle Walsh, Paddy Walsh's daughter? Sure I knew your dad. He was the toughest cop I ever met. Every cop in this city would trust him to have their back in any situation. I'm sorry for your loss. It was a great loss for all of us."

"Thanks Sir. He always spoke highly of you," she said, shaking his hand and breaking into an infectious grin. "He used to say you were a good enough detective that you would still be a good patrol cop."

"Sounds like your dad," he laughed. "But you are still calling me sir and that is going to be awkward because I am going to call you Nicky. You saw something in the pictures, didn't you Nicky?"

"What are they Detective?" She asked, looking back at the wall.

"Well, this is a need to know only deal but I am going to trust you. The three photos are of folded pieces of paper left on three different murder victims within the last six days. One of them was the case at Carnegie Hall that you and your partner caught. We believe these three graphs are enough to link the murders together. Now we are trying to figure out what they mean. We have had a lot of guesses but so far no answers."

"What do you see Officer Walsh?"

"I see games of chess. At first I thought maybe chess, maybe checkers, but if you look at the second game, the two circles are in the same starting position that kings would be in on a chess board. They are in the same column at opposite ends of the board from each other. Of course all the squares are white and the white king would be on a black square. So if you colored in all the appropriate black squares it would work. Also, I can't explain why there are no other game pieces on the board in game two. But if I had to guess, I would say chess."

Paul Worton looked at the young officer, then the photos, then back to Nicky Walsh. He knew the answer before he asked the question.

"How can you be so sure?"

"Oh, I have played chess all my life. Chess club geek in high school. In fact, I did my thesis on chess in grad school, if you can believe that. I still play speed chess with whoever shows up down in Central Park, when I get the chance." She said.

Worton turned away as he spoke.

"Don't go anywhere Officer Walsh, you are temporarily assigned to me. I will have my boss call your boss."

"People! Those photos on the wall may well be chess games," he said loud enough to get everyone's attention. "Morales, find me the best chess expert in the city."

Worton pressed a button on his cell phone.

"Lieutenant. Worton here. Hey Boss, can you to get a patrol officer assigned to this case? Yeah, her name is Nicky Walsh, Paddy Walsh's daughter. Well, she took one look at those papers the killer left and said they were chess games so I would like to keep her around if possible. Okay. Thanks, I will be in touch." Worton hung up and glanced, one more time, at the images on the wall.

"What is this psycho up to?" He said out loud.

* * *

The moment Nicky Walsh said the word, chess Paul Worton knew she was right or at least that the folded pieces of paper represented either chessboards or checkerboards. It seemed so obvious now. Not musical notes, but pieces on a game board. Worton played chess on occasion, knew how the pieces moved and basic strategy. But that was it. He was no expert on the game.

Worton studied the photocopies on his desk.

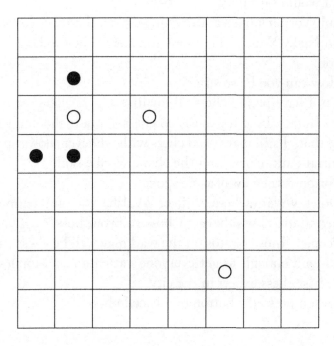

The King's Gambit

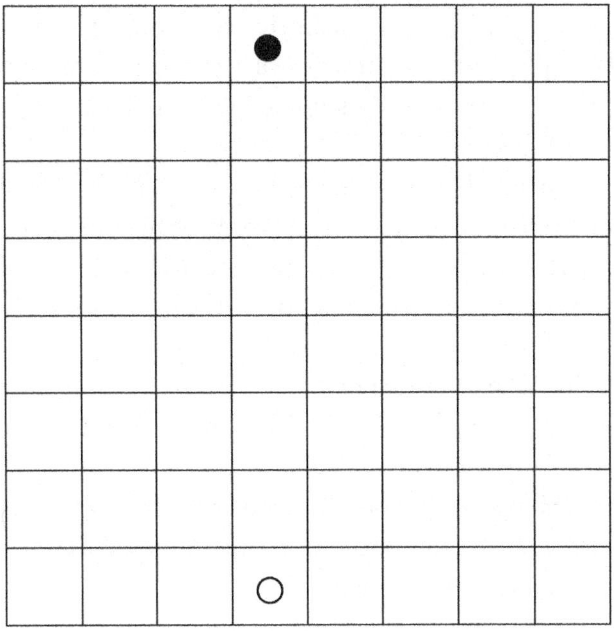

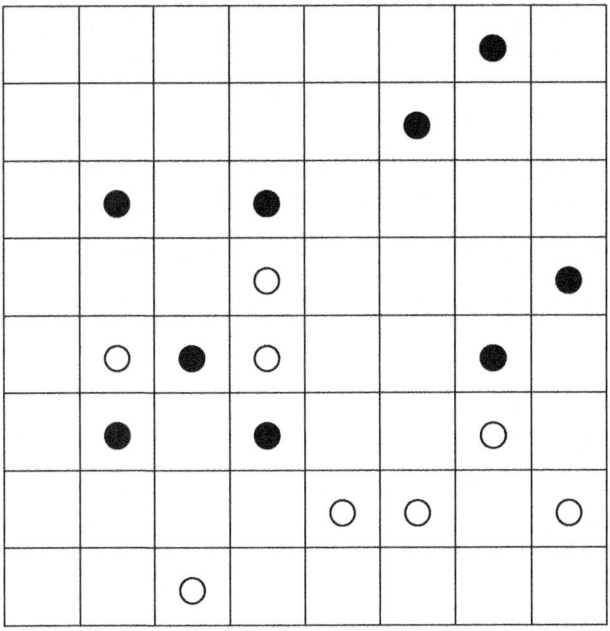

He wondered why the kings in game two were still in their original positions. More importantly, why would a killer kill three different people and leave images of three different chess games behind? They were clues to something and the killer obviously wanted them found.

Worton needed help, and he knew it. Nicky Walsh knew chess and knew police work, she would stay on the Task Force for now. Detective Morales was in contact with a New York City Grandmaster who was reputed to be the most renowned chess player in the United States. They would meet with him later that evening. But Worton was not satisfied. He had one more person in mind. Someone he could trust someone who knew chess. Someone he could rely on.

Worton hit speed dial on his cell phone. How long will it take me to convince him that I am serious, he thought? After two rings a strong but raspy voice answered.

"Nuge here."

"Hey, Nuge it's me, Paul."

"Hey, Paul we gonna play today? Don't tell me you're scared an old coot like me will kick your ass," the voice said.

"No, I can't play today."

"Fine, you chicken. Hey, guess what? Remember I told you about my new, pop-up book idea?"

"Yeah, Nuge, that's great. You can give me the low down on it later."

"Jeez! Sorry. Someone is having a bad day. You pissed at me?"

Worton let out a deep sigh.

"No, Nuge, I am not pissed at you. I need your help, Buddy. It's a case I am working on."

"Really? Why me? You pulling my leg like usual?" Nuge asked.

"No, and I need you like right now. How soon can you get here?"

"You sound serious."

"I am dead serious. Get here as soon as you can. I told them downstairs to let you up. I am hanging up. I have twenty more calls to make. See you soon." Paul hung up the phone and looked at his watch.

"Damn! I have to call Lori."

* * *

After a shower and a short nap, Michael made a quick breakfast consisting of a ham and cheese omelet, with toast and coffee. Now he felt completely refreshed and relaxed.

He sat at the easel surrounded by the gray stone walls of the hidden room.

It was time to ratchet things up. First, a little help for the young journalist.

He downloaded a close up picture of Vincent Antonelli's ornate baton into his e-mail attachments, typed a few words and sent it on its way. If he had Andy Wiley pegged correctly, the evening news shows and early editions would be very interesting.

Michael checked his game board and glanced at the remaining clues secured inside eight zip locks bags. His eyes rose and fixed on a poster on the far wall.

Bobby Fischer stood tall in the picture, looming over a chess board. Fischer's opponent seemed almost to cower in his seat. He wore a black suit with his arms folded and the fingers of one hand holding his chin. His eyes were alive, almost gleaming with the look of a conqueror.

Michael took a deep breath to slow his heart beat. He was positive that Fischer knew the winning move in the picture. He was waiting for his victim to step into his trap. The giant image always left him excited and rejuvenated.

He shut the light out and left the room to get dressed. He had places to go, things to do, and one more person to contact.

Lori Worton was back at work after a gorgeous forty-eight hour respite at the beach house in Montauk. She was totally refreshed and golden brown from two days of baking in the sun with a book in one hand and a pina colada in the other. The only drawback was Paul's absence. The rest of the crew arrived on time and the party started immediately. It continued until late Sunday afternoon. They drank too much, ate too much and played every game they could think of. But, of course, in the world of vacationing people, Monday morning always looms its ugly head, and all too soon they were packing up and saying goodbye.

The store was full, with ten or twelve customers wading through shelves and tables of rustic wall coverings, country collectibles, candles and napkins, along with selected colonial furniture and antiques. But Lori found it hard to concentrate on work. She had not seen Paul in six days and she was glad Melanie and Terry were working with her.

He had called twice. She knew from what he said, and from the news reports, that he would probably not be home for some time. They had been married twenty-one years and, because of the job, there were many times when they did not spend the night together. She also knew that being away from each other for any length of time was not going to work for either of them. He would call her today, and they would find a way to meet. They always did. Lori could not wait to see him. These times apart made her feel like a school girl anticipating prom night. Knowing it would be romantic, but not sure where they would end up or how far the romance would go.

She laughed as she made her way to a customer rummaging through various antiques in a back corner of the store. She wasn't so sure about prom night, but she was pretty sure how far things would go whenever she saw her husband again.

"Can I help you, Sir?" She said to a tall older gentleman who had been in the antique section for some time.

The King's Gambit

* * *

Robert Nugent walked up the stone steps leading to the entrance of the 18th Precinct building, which housed the Midtown North Police Precinct. He had been friends with Paul Worton for ten years, yet had never set foot in his place of business. They met at The Body Works Fitness Center where both men were long time members. Paul was in a full sweat, hitting balls on an empty racquetball court when "The Nuge" showed up looking for a game. The Nuge never let Worton forget how he tried to beg out of the game, not wanting to embarrass the old man, before losing three straight games without scoring more than five points. They still played once or twice a week, depending on Paul's schedule, but the games were always a toss-up now. Worton had worked hard on his game but, when he won, Nuge would always remind him that he was beating an eighty two year old man.

Robert Nugent was born in Brooklyn, in 1924, and still lived there. He enlisted two days after graduating from high school at the age of eighteen. His dad wanted him to use his asthma attacks to get himself declared 4-F, but "The Nuge" hid the doctor's note during the physical and spent the next four years surviving the brutal island hopping campaign across the Pacific. Using money from the G.I. bill, he graduated from N.Y.U. at the top of his class with a business degree. For the next fifty years, "The Nuge" was a fixture in every corner of the advertisement and entertainment business in New York City. His ads appeared in magazines, newspapers and on billboards. He made commercials and movie trailers. He was involved in the production of three Broadway shows and two television sitcoms, not to mention serving as publicity man for two political campaigns and various celebrities. Even now, he had not slowed down. On top of playing tennis or racquetball twice a week, Nuge made his way out to the island at least once a week to play golf. "The Nuge" was never seen without his trusty manila folder tucked under his arm. Inside the envelope were all of the newest ideas, from doing the advertising for a fledgling woman's basketball team, to a first draft for a pop-up children's book.

Paul Worton did not call his old buddy for any of those reasons. He called "The Nuge" because he knew Robert Nugent was an avid chess player and, when he was focused, one of the sharpest minds he had ever encountered. The trick would be to get him focused.

All "The Nuge" knew was that he could not wait to show Paul the newest draft of his book idea.

* * *

No matter what he was into, Paul Worton was always happier after he heard Lori's voice, even if only for a moment. That moment was just enough to remind him that his real world existed out there with her, and no matter what he ran into on the job, things would be okay. Today's call had been no different.

"Hey Baby! I was beginning to worry that you forgot about me." Lori said, answering almost before the first ring ended.

"No chance of that Kiddo. What's up?" he said.

"It's been almost a week since I've seen you. Any chance you can get away for a couple of hours? I promise you won't be sorry," she whispered.

"I'm meeting with the Task Force at ten o'clock. I might be able to slip away around midnight. But you have to promise not to tell my wife. She gets really jealous," he joked.

"I heard she shuts you off when you are a wise guy. So you better hope she doesn't hear you say mean things about her. She may just have a headache when you two meet," she countered.

Paul laughed out loud.

"Come on Lori, you know you can't threaten me with that any more than I could threaten you. So let's stop fooling around. Do you want to stay in the city tonight?" he asked.

"Do you remember I told you that Rita was flying over to meet Dean in France? His conference ended Friday, and they decided to meet and do Europe while he was over there. Well, I told her I would check on the place and pick up her mail for the next two weeks. We could spend the night there. Do you remember where they live?"

"Yeah, somewhere down around Gramercy Park. We went to a New Year's party there one year. Real nice place on the third floor. You would have to give me the exact address," he replied.

"It's the second building up from the corner of East 21st and Lexington. It's number three seventeen on the third floor. In case you don't remember, Rita and Dean's last name is Sanders. Just press the button and I'll buzz you in," Lori told him. "I'll grab something quick for us to eat and drink. I can't wait to see you Baby."

"Me too, Kiddo," He said. "I'll call if anything changes. If not, I will see you as soon as I can get there."

"Ok. I gotta run. The store is swamped today. I love you. Bye."

Worton heard the click and was still smiling when he hooked his phone to his belt and started down the hall to a meeting with "Nuge", Officer Nicky Walsh and a New York City Chess Grandmaster that Morales had contacted. He had one thought on his mind. He could not wait until midnight.

His hand was still on the phone when it rang. He shook his head as the grin on his face grew.

"I know you are anxious, Kiddo, but you are going to have to wait until midnight to have your way with me."

The male voice on the other end stopped him in mid-stride.

"I am sorry to disappoint you Detective, but unless you are a much better player than I anticipated, we will not be meeting any time soon."

Worton moved quickly back to the squad room, and pushed the door open with his hip. He grabbed a New York City phone book from the nearest desk and threw it on the floor in the middle of the room with a resounding bang. The noise startled every detective and police officer in the room. Some reached for weapons and some ducked, but they all looked up to see Worton with his cell phone to his ear, and his right index finger to his lips asking for quiet.

"You know my name. I am at a disadvantage. Can I ask who I am speaking to?" As he asked the question, he pulled up a chair, grabbed a pencil and piece of paper and started writing. He would try to record every word the man said .

"Well, you are the detective. I think I would be doing you a disservice if I did not leave you something to detect," the man replied.

"You said player. What kind of game do you envision us playing?" Worton asked.

"I think you have that figured out by now Detective. The powers that be would never put you in charge of a situation of this magnitude if you were not the best they have. They always cover their butts in these high profile cases. They will want to protect their image with the public and you are the man they have put their faith in. Congratulations, Detective,"

"From where I sit this is no game. Why did you call me? What exactly is it that you want?"

"Good question. I thought it would only be fair to acknowledge my opponent. I have done that. You have my opening moves detective. Good luck."

The line went dead.

* * *

It was an hour later that Paul Worton strode back down the same hallway to his previously planned meeting. A lot had happened in the interim. Immediately after the call, he sent word that the meeting would be delayed. Then he had Detective Morales take his statement. He wanted every word of his conversation with the killer on the record while it was fresh in his mind. The call was traced to a phone booth in Soho. The elderly woman using the phone to call her daughter left a little scared and very angry with the crime scene unit that descended upon her. They dusted everything, and swept the area for any possible evidence, but Worton had no illusions that this subject would be that careless. Things went from bad to worse when Anthony walked into Lt. Copeland's office as Worton was relating the details of the call to his boss.

"You guys are going to want to see this," Anthony said, walking to the television set on the far wall and switching it on. He quickly scrolled down to the channel he wanted and stepped back.

Anchorwoman Karen Meadows was sitting at her normal perch behind the Channel 4 News desk, speaking straight into the camera.

"As we promised earlier in our broadcast, we have an exclusive report from investigative reporter Andy Wiley, in connection with the shocking murder of renowned New York Philharmonic conductor Vincent Antonelli."

"Andy?" she said, turning to her left.

The camera swung in the same direction and found Andy Wiley sitting at a similar desk. He looked calm and relaxed, and nodded acknowledgment without ever turning towards his colleague. He showed no sign of the adrenaline coursing through his body. He had waited his whole career for this moment. With as much concocted concern as he could muster, he spoke into the camera.

"Good evening. We here at Channel 4 have recently received shocking details related to the death of Vincent Antonelli. We have learned that Mr. Antonelli was stabbed to death somewhere between the hours of 11:00 p.m. and 1:00 a.m. in the main promenade of the famed Carnegie Hall building, a little over a week ago. We have also learned that the killer used the famous conductor's own personalized baton as a murder weapon. It is reported that the victim was tied to a chair and then stabbed through the neck, and left on display only to be found the next morning by a janitor. It is said that the authorities are exhausting all leads and leaving no stone unturned, although at this time they have very few clues and no real suspects. We have learned, however, that the Mayor and the Police Commissioner have met to discuss where the investigation will go from here. A press conference is planned for tomorrow morning. Vincent Antonelli was not just an extremely talented musician, but was connected to some very high profile people, not just in New York City, but across the country. We will do our best to keep the public informed on this subject as we learn more. I am Andy Wiley, reporting for Channel 4 News. Now back to Karen at our news desk."

Lt. Tim Copeland pushed the off button on the remote and sat back in his chair. He looked at Paul Worton.

"Where did that come from?" he asked.

"No idea. As far as I know, no one but the people in this department know how he died, no less what the weapon was."

"Well someone is talking, and I want to know who. I'm telling you now, if the leak is coming from one of our people, they will be done here. I don't care who it is. Do you understand me?" Copeland said.

Worton left the squad room knowing two things. Tim Copeland had his back, but he was already taking heat from all directions while trying to protect the Task Force. Department heavy hitters all the way up to the Mayor's office wanted answers. Every media outlet had The Carnegie Hall murder as its lead story, and he knew the scrutiny would double when they found out there was a serial killer on the loose. And they would find out.

Andy Wiley was a problem. If the killer could get Paul's cell phone number, he could easily contact the media. Worton was pretty sure where the kid from Channel 4 got his info. Anthony and Morales would question him first thing in the morning. Their orders were to bring him in if he refused to cooperate.

He knew that Copeland had talked to people in the Criminal Assessment Unit, along with the Behavioral Science Unit of the

F.B.I. They were in the process of trying to put together a profile of the killer. Worton also knew they would need more information than they now had, to get a true reading on this guy.

He needed answers and he needed them quickly.

As Paul Worton opened the door to the conference room, he hoped the three people inside would have some clue to those answers.

* * *

Chess expert Victor Menchenko, Officer Nicky Walsh and "The Nuge" all looked up when he entered. The three looked to be from different planets. Nicky Walsh sat at the end of a long table. She had changed into faded jeans, a bright red tee and a brown leather jacket, and she looked to be at least fifty years younger than the two men. Paul Worton chuckled. "The Nuge" sat mid-table looking like he always did, just a little bit crazy and disheveled. He wore a crumpled baseball hat, a t-shirt with "*life is good*" stenciled on the front, baggy shorts and sneakers. Victor Menchenko was close to the same age as "The Nuge", but couldn't have been more different if he tried. From head to toe, he was perfectly groomed and dressed. He wore a tailored suit and his white hair and mustache were trimmed to perfection. He was pacing the far end of the room when Worton entered.

"Sorry to keep you waiting. We had a sort of emergency crop up. Mr. Menchenko, I am Detective Paul Worton. This is Officer Nicky Walsh and Robert Nugent," he continued as they all shook hands. "Let me explain why you are here. Our research led us to you, Mr Menchenko. We needed to find the best chess mind we could, as quickly as we could, and your name kept coming up. Officer Walsh is part of my investigative team and Mr. Nugent is an old crony of mine, who I believe can be of help on the case in question." Worton paused for a moment.

"Please don't take this the wrong way because it is not meant as an insult. But if you decide to stay, I must have your word that what you see or hear in this room will not leave this room. You can't discuss this case, even with family members."

"I am not sure why I am here detective, but I am willing to hear you out." The great Grandmaster said. "The Nuge" just nodded his head and waited.

Worton pressed a button on the department's new Landro projection system. Enlarged images of three sheets of paper appeared on the wall.

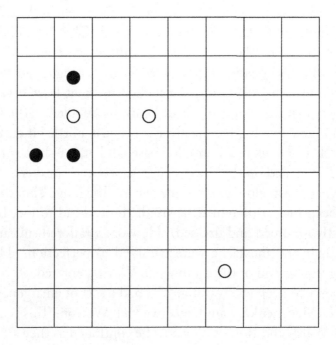

The King's Gambit

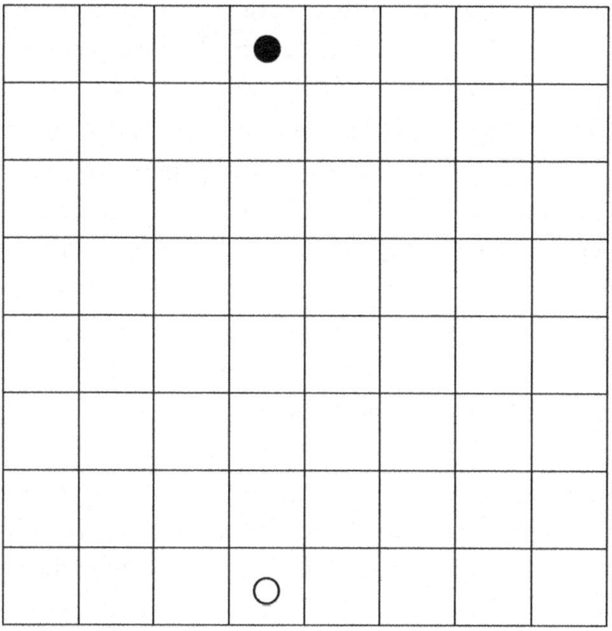

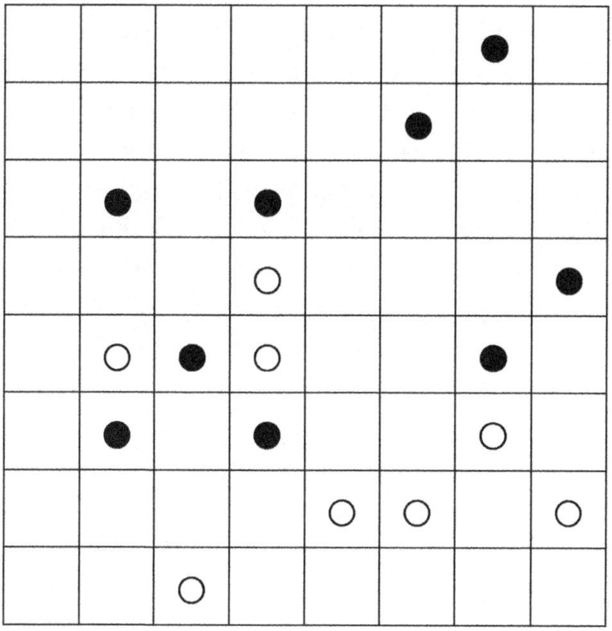

"The media and the public believe we have a high profile murder case on our hands, and we do. But we have much more than that going on here. We are dealing with a serial killer. He has killed three times already, and he left a folded piece of paper on each victim. The images from those papers are projected here on the wall. We believe the killer is leaving clues behind in some sort of twisted test to challenge us to stop him." Worton pointed to Nicky.

"Officer Walsh took one look at these clues and pointed out they could be chess games depending on which piece is which and where the kings are. It seems she has had some experience with the game. I, on the other hand, am a novice. Mr. Nugent is an old friend whose opinion I value greatly, and it so-happens that he plays chess every day in one form or another. I am hoping he can add some insight. That brings me to you, Mr. Menchenko. I told my people to find the finest chess mind in New York City. Your name kept coming up. Your credentials speak for themselves. U.S. Champion, Grand Master, and President of the most prestigious chess club in the city. Mr. Menchenko, you are here, if you so choose, to review whatever evidence we have pertaining to chess and to teach us all you can about the game. I'm not talking about how the pieces move, we have all played chess, I am talking about what makes great players tick. How they think the game."

Victor Menchenko smiled and tugged on the vest of his three piece suit.

"That will not be easy detective," he said with just a hint of a European accent. "Every great player is different. They never just play the board. They play the opponent and the surroundings as if they were intricate parts of the game. He or she will think as many as ten or fifteen moves ahead, both his moves and his opponents. Opening moves, defenses and end games, all have names representing great masters of the past. All good players know these moves, instantly. Many great matches are decided by the demeanor, or will, of the man rather than the pieces on the board." Menchenko paused to look at the wall.

The King's Gambit

"Your young detective is correct. These so-called clues are chess games. After studying them and working out various scenarios, I believe games one and three show completed games. That is, allowing that the circles in certain squares represent mated kings." He picked up a black magic marker lying on the table and stepped to the wall. He then drew an X in a square on the first board.

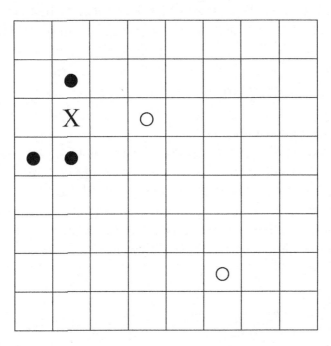

"If this X represents the white King, that player would have to resign his King and the game. Screen two is different, if it is a chess board. The only pieces showing are the opposing kings in their original starting position.

The three others in the room were impressed. Worton heard all he needed to hear, Menchenko could help the case. Nicky Walsh wondered where Menchenko's knowledge could lead them in the investigation and whether what she learned would improve her game if she ever got to play again. "The Nuge" just wanted to play a game against him. He would probably get killed in six moves or so but at least he would get to play a Grandmaster. Who knows, he thought, Rocky beat Apollo Creed so anything is possible.

"Ok," Worton said. "What I need the three of you to do is spend as much time as you can in this room. I need to find some clue from these pieces of paper. We agree these are chess games, at least two of them anyway. He is definitely talking to us but we need to know what he is saying. I will get whatever you need to be comfortable. You can wait until tomorrow if you want, but my feeling is the longer we flounder with this, the more people will die." He paused to write a number on a yellow pad of paper.

"I am leaving my cell phone number. Call any time. Anything you come up with might help. I have been doing this a long time and you never know what breaks a case open. I have to run an errand but I will be back before dawn. If you can, I would like to meet with you tomorrow morning say around eight. Is that good for everyone?"

"I am glad to help if I can detective. But I am a very busy man as you can imagine. I will give of my time when possible but, I have a prior engagement tonight," Menchenko said. "I will, of course, stay as long as possible and try to stop in tomorrow."

Worton nodded and looked at Nuge.

"What about you Nuge? I know you have fifty different irons in the fire, but I could use your help." For the first time in their relationship his old friend gave him a straight answer.

"Whatever you need Paul. I'll do what I can."

It was another hour before Worton left the conference room. Everything that could be done had been put in motion. There was nothing more he could do tonight. It was time to get away, time to see Lori. He headed out the back door to his car. Anyone watching Paul Worton leaving the Precinct would assume he was a cop.

A few blocks up on the other side of the city, anyone watching the old man leave the back entrance of the 64th Street brownstone would have no idea they were watching a cold blooded killer stalking his next victim.

* * *

It was nearly two a.m. before "The Nuge" headed home promising to return sometime the following morning. Before Victor Menchenko left for the evening, the three designated chess experts talked long and hard about the game itself and how it might pertain to the killer's plan. While the Grandmaster and Nuge discussed every strategy and nuance, Nicky Walsh took notes, listened and learned. Menchenko seemed stunned by "The Nuge's" knowledge and understanding of the game, while Nicky learned more listening to the two men than she ever did sitting at a chess board.

Now the two men were gone and she sat starring at the clues on the wall. Something about the first game bothered her. She had seen it somewhere before, she was sure of it.

Nicky walked down to the squad room. It was a quiet night and a skeleton crew was on duty. The six men in the room never looked up when she entered.

"Hey you guys. Do you know if there is a chess set in the building?"

"A chess set?

"Yeah, a chess set you know knights, kings, bishops, pawns." She said.

"No, not that I know of, but there are some games down in the coffee room. Cribbage board, checkers, cards."

"Checkers? That will do. Thanks."

She quickly found the old worn game box and headed back to the conference room.

* * *

Paul Worton lay on his back, watching the gray shadows of furniture and wall coverings softly illuminated by a glow filtering in from the bathroom night light. Times like this made it hard for him to rationalize a job that found him matching wits with a maniac who wanted to play a game, where the life and death of innocent people hung in the balance.

An hour earlier, Lori met him at the door to their friend's apartment. She had a meal of lasagna and salad waiting, with the table set and candles lit. They ate and talked over a couple of glasses of wine. She told of the weekend at the beach and he filled her in on the case. She also reported on the antics of their fourteen year old daughter. He had not seen Jackie in almost a week and it took a while to cover every one of the different directions her teenage life was going. He heard about the beach, her job at the library, babysitting, softball practice, shopping, and of course, the boyfriend she still denied having.

He did not remember moving to the couch or falling asleep there, but he did remember her waking him. She was kissing his lips and she was naked. She took his hand and led him to the bedroom.

He turned his head to her and inhaled deeply. Her scent was enough to arouse him. Was it the combination of her perfume, her soap, her body? He did not know but he knew her scent and he loved it.

Lori's breath was soft but deep, where her head rested on his shoulder. He could feel the swell of her breast and the curve of her body along his left side. Her left arm draped across his chest as her left leg straddled his thigh.

The room was warm and the bed covers were on the floor at the end of the bed, with only a single white sheet covering them from the waist down.

Paul let his fingers graze the thin gold chain and the soft jet black hair at the base of her neck. Slowly, he slid his hand down her back brushing her smooth, darkly tanned, olive skin. His touch followed the line of her backbone to the small hollow at the base of her spine, just above the swell of her bottom. His fingers drifted lower and traced the lines of the tattoo on her left hip. In his mind, he could see the small, rose colored cupid heart with his initials printed inside. It had been a tenth anniversary present and he never tired of touching it. She stirred at his touch and leaned her thigh even further into his body, causing the reaction he knew would come. She woke with a smile and crawled up to bite his neck.

Paul glanced at the clock on the nightstand. It was four in the morning and he would have to leave soon, but not just yet.

He rolled on top of her, kissing her deeply and letting her feel the hardness of his body.

* * *

GAME 4

July 20th

"One of the variables is your opponent's psychology. So you attack a person's psychological weaknesses. Put him under tremendous strain. Push him to consume his energy."

Shelby Lyman

Detective Anthony Austin worked out every morning at the Police Academy Training Facility, half-way down 20th Street between 2nd and 3rd Avenues. The entrance to the building looked like a garage door with a grate across the front. Anthony was always the first to arrive and this day he was even earlier. He was a bit of a legend at the Academy, having set a record for completing the obstacle course on his first try, eight years earlier. Now, when available, he was the Academy's best instructor. Anthony loved any kind of physical competition. He worked religiously in the weight room, played basketball three times a week and jogged at least five miles on the days in between.

The section of 20th Street was still dark and almost deserted when Anthony jogged up to the steel gate. The city was starting to stir, but the street was empty except for a few transients sleeping under their cardboard blankets, next to beat up shopping carts holding their every worldly possession. He knew he had maybe two hours for a good workout and a shower before he had to meet Morales and go pick up the kid reporter from Channel 4.

Anthony unlocked the grate and slid it to the right hand wall. He lifted the garage door and stepped into the shadows. He was barely able to make out the police van on the left side of the entrance and the glassed in security shack on the right.

Maybe it was the noise from the grate or maybe the shadowy darkness. Maybe because he just wasn't expecting anything. He never noticed a movement or a sound before the sharp blade plunged through his back and into his spinal cord. The attack left him paralyzed from the waist down. He only stayed on his feet, as he was dragged deeper into the darkness of the garage, because of his attacker's strength. Anthony tried to fight with his upper body but he could not turn. He never felt the knife come out as the man turned him around but he felt it as it re-entered his body from the front right, through his spleen. His body jerked and he grabbed his assailant's arms. As the man lowered him to the ground, he knew he was dying. He looked up at the face of a grizzled old homeless man.

Michael Mueller looked into the eyes of the young detective and was surprised to see no fear there. It seemed more like disappointment which confused him for a moment. He did not linger long. He took a plastic bag from his pocket and removed the small folded piece of paper. He tucked the paper under the collar of Anthony's NYPD tee shirt, patted Anthony on the chest, left the garage and walked up 20th Street.

Anthony watched him go and then watched the pool of dark, almost black, blood grow next to his right arm. How many times had he seen a corpse lying in a pool like that? Now he was the corpse. What would Paul say? What would he think? I was careless. I screwed up. I have to let him know I tried.

Anthony reached out as far as he could.

* * *

Nicky Walsh was sound asleep sitting with her arms cradling her head on the conference room table, when Paul Worton entered the room. It was 7:00 a.m. and he had been in the building awhile. He came in early to review the case file and was waiting to hear from Jose and Anthony. They were due around eight with Andrew Wiley, the reporter from Channel 4. In the squad room he asked what time his chess team had called it a night and was surprised to learn that Officer Walsh was still in the building.

He looked over the sleeping girl's shoulder at a checker board by her elbow. He then glanced at the images still projected on the wall. The checker board was set up exactly like the page from the first murder.

He touched her shoulder and spoke.

"Nicky."

She woke with a start, her hand falling instinctively to her side even though her shield and weapon were on the table in front of her.

"Oh, sorry Detective I wasn't sure where I was for a moment."

"Call me Paul or you're fired," he said smiling. "What the hell are you still doing here?"

"Well, to tell the truth, home is just a one room walk-up. I am really more comfortable here."

"What's with the checkers, Nicky?" He asked sitting down.

"Well, after Mr. Menchenko put the X's up there, something clicked. I knew I had seen that first game somewhere. So I thought if I could set it up it might help me remember. I'm very visual. It always helps me to see things in reality," she answered.

"I'm the same way," he said. "Did it help?"

"Yeah, I think so. Do you know who Bobby Fischer was?"

"Sure, the crazy bastard who hates the U. S. but won the world championship, against that Russian guy, back in the seventies," Worton said. "Everyone loved him then, but now he's a radical recluse living in Iceland, I think."

"That's him. It was Boris Spassky that he defeated. I was a bit of a nut on that match when I first started playing. In fact, the thesis I told you about centered on their 1972 World Championship match," she said with an infectious smile. "Anyway, Spassky won game one of the match and Fischer won game three. Well, the pieces on page one are in exactly the same places as the pieces were at the end of game one in 1972."

Worton looked from the board to the wall twice.

"No shit," he said. "You're sure?"

"Positive."

Worton stood and walked to the wall, staring at the images. He took a deep breath.

"What about games two and three?" He asked turning back to Nicky.

"Well, game two was a forfeit. Fischer was pissed about cameras in the room and never showed up, so Spassky won. Fischer won game three and I believe those pieces ended up in the same places as the ones on the wall."

Worton stepped closer to the wall and put his finger on the black dot at the top of page two.

"So, if you colored in the black squares, this could be game two. If the kings never moved, they would be here and here." He said moving his finger to the white circle at the bottom of the page.

"That is exactly right, sir, uh, Paul."

"So what the hell does that mean? What is he telling us?" Worton asked, almost too quietly to hear.

* * *

One hour later, the conference room was humming with activity. Upon his arrival, Victor Menchenko immediately confirmed Nicky Walsh's assertion that images one and three were, indeed, exact replicas of the final position of game pieces in games one and three of the Fischer-Spassky chess match of 1972. It took a few minutes to calm the Grandmaster down and get him to move on from reprimanding himself for not recognizing the checkmated games, instantly. Now, Menchenko was telling every detail he could remember about the most famous chess match in history.

In the meantime, Paul Worton had detectives from the Homicide Task Force pouring over every book and article ever written about the match. They needed times and dates, wins and losses, names and pictures, anything and everything that might give some clue to what was driving the killer's madness. He had a small lead and he was running with it as hard as he could.

The conference room door opened and Nicky Walsh stepped in looking totally refreshed. Her hair was still wet from her shower and she had changed clothes. "The Nuge" was right behind her and looked a little disheveled, as usual, and a little out of breath. He pushed past Officer Walsh with a quick apology.

"Pauley, Pauley! I think I got something. Well maybe. I don't know." He said.

"The Nuge" moved quickly down the long table toward Paul Worton and Victor Menchenko holding out a manila folder clutched in his hand.

"Easy "Nuge", calm down and go slowly," Paul said, holding up his hand. "We're all listening. What have you got?"

"The Nuge" looked around the room. It was full of people working on various parts of the case but they were all watching him now. He looked at his good friend pleadingly. "Maybe it is nothing, Pauly."

"You never know what will break a case, "Nuge". It could be anything. Tell me what you have." Worton said.

"Well, I took some pictures yesterday. You know I always carry my digital camera in my pocket," he explained. "Well, before I left I took pictures of the city map, with the three murder places. What do you guys call 'em, murder scenes? And I took pictures, of the three messages the guy left."

"Nuge", you took crime scene photos home?" Worton asked incredulously.

"Well, yeah Paul but I didn't show anyone."

"Not the point, "Nuge", but go on."

"Well, you know there are nine avenues and nine cross streets in the city, right?"

"Well, I guess I knew that," Paul said. "What about it?"

As he spoke, Victor Menchenko let out a gasp.

"Oh my God!" He said. "Sixty-four squares! Of course!" Worton looked from him to "The Nuge" and back.

"Sixty-four squares. What the hell is he talking about?" Worton asked.

"The Nuge" took a sheet of paper from his folder.

9th Ave.	8th Ave.	7th Ave.	6th Ave.	5th Ave.	4th Ave.	3rd Ave.	2nd Ave.
96th St.							
86th St.							
72nd St.							
57th St.		Carnegie Hall					
42nd St.							
34th St.							
23rd St.							
9th Ave. 14th St.	8th Ave.	7th Ave.	6th Ave	5th Ave.	4th Ave.	3rd Ave.	2nd Ave

"This is the city. Just the nine avenues and nine cross streets drawn in. Everything else has been removed, leaving 64 squares which is the same number of squares on a chess board," he said and reached back into the folder. "These three pages are the same as the first with the streets and avenues. But on each one, I added the circles and dots from each murder. I'm not sure what it means. I think he is using the city as a chess board."

A long, stunned, silence filled the room. Finally, Paul spoke.

"Let me see if I have this straight. We have a guy out there who is killing people. He is leaving clues that show completed chess moves from thirty-four years ago. He is killing them in certain parts of the city, which he is using as his chess board and the scenes of the crime match the squares where Kings were checkmated in 1972?"

"Or killed." Nicky Walsh said.

"Killed? What do you mean killed?" Paul asked.

"In chess, a mated King has to surrender. He can't move or fight. He might as well be dead." Victor Merchenko said.

"So he is killing his version of kings? Head of the Philharmonic, Head of the Union, Top Gun at the Arts Academy," Nicky Walsh mused. The question was rhetorical. Twelve people sat around the conference table in silence, trying to digest what they had just heard.

The tension broke when Detective Morales opened the door.

"Hey Paul I got that news guy, Wiley, out here and he ain't too happy. Snatched him up at the *Daily News* parking garage. People at Channel 4 clued me in that Wiley had an interview over there this morning. I was waiting for him when he got there. Kinda strong-armed him, words, not physical. Anyway, he sounds like he is going to lawyer up before we get anything out of him," Jose paused. "Why so serious? What's going on?"

"We have had quite a morning and night, I guess. I'll fill you in later," Paul answered. "OK. The people in this room need to piece this together and have a synopsis of what they think this guy is doing and, if possible, what he is going to do next. We need a game plan people, and we need it now."

"OK, Jose, let's go get Anthony and find out who's been talking to our media man."

"Anthony never showed Paul. I called his cell and his home phone. Finally, I went and got the kid myself," Jose said. "He's probably hung over at some chick's place. You know Anthony."

Paul Worton had his hand on the doorknob. He stopped and turned to face Jose Morales. "That's not Anthony's M.O. He always shows. Even if he can hardly walk, sick or hung over, he shows up."

Before Detective Morales could answer, the knob turned in Worton's hand and Tim Copeland pushed his way in. His boss's eyes met Worton's and the look sent a chill through Worton's spine.

"I need to talk to you Paul"

"What's up, Boss?"

"Let's step outside Paul." Tim Copeland said, putting his hand on Worton's shoulder.

"No, Lieutenant, let's do this here." He could tell by Copeland's tone and the look in his eye, that he would not like what he was about to hear. But he wanted to hear it here and he wanted his team to hear it. Detective Lieutenant Tim Copeland knew Worton well. They had worked together for fifteen years. It would do no good to argue with him.

"What's going on?" Worton asked him again. Copeland looked at the faces in the room and took a deep breath.

"Detective Anthony Austin is dead. He was stabbed to death at the entrance to the Police Academy Training Center on 20th Street around 5:00 or 5:30 this morning. No witnesses. Morning shift perimeter detail officer found him."

Silence hung in the room. Everyone except "The Nuge" and Victor Menchenko, knew Anthony. He was young, outgoing and a friend. He was one of them. Jose sat down in the nearest chair and ran his hands through his hair. Anthony was not only a partner he was more like a younger brother. Tears welled in Jose's eyes. Nicky Walsh thought of the young man with the infectious smile, who had blatantly checked her out when they first met but, somehow, did not offend her.

Tim Copeland stared at Paul Worton's face. It seemed the detective had stopped breathing. His eyes were fixed on the wall.

"It's him. He did this. The chess guy. He wanted to get my attention. That is why he called me. That's why he contacted Wiley and that's why he killed Anthony." Worton said to no one in particular. "Well, he has my attention now."

"He left a message Paul." Copeland said.

"Yeah, I figured another chess board to add to the collection." Worton spit out.

"No Paul, not the chess board. Anthony left a message for you. Not sure what it means but nothing's been touched," Copeland said. "We can just take pictures if you want."

"A message?" Worton asked.

"Yeah. You need to see it as soon as possible."

Paul Worton turned to the people in the room. "Find out where the Police Academy Training Center is on our city chess board and where the King was at the end of Fischer's game four. I have a feeling you will find it right in the middle of that square."

Worton walked out the door, followed closely by Copeland, Morales and Nicky Walsh.

* * *

More than fifty NYPD personnel were inside the dark garage entrance to the Police Academy Training Center. Cops from Crime Scene, the M. E.'s office, Academy personnel and cops who heard the call were at the scene. None of them were near the fallen detective. Even Copeland, Morales and Nicky Walsh left Paul Worton alone with Anthony. His face was white now and his body rigid. The pool of blood was black and seemed enormous. It always seemed like too much blood for one body. And this was Anthony's blood. Thank God his eyes were closed, Worton thought. He knelt on one knee next to the young detective. Worton was in pain: physical pain. His stomach hurt and blood pounded in his head.

Anthony was dead. Worton could not help him now. He knew the boy died because he was part of Worton's team. He would blame himself later. Anthony was at his best in a crime scene and he had tried as much as he could to help with this one. The one he died in the middle of.

Anthony's legs were splayed straight out from his body and his head was turned to his right. His right arm stretched from his body toward the wall. The fingers of his right hand rested on the floor, at the end of a message written in his own blood.

P.W. - TALL STRONG U.S.
NOT BUM   YOUNG
MY L HAND
SORRY   STUPID

Worton rose and stepped back, wiping tears from his eyes. He did not care who knew he was hurting.

"Okay, now this is personal. Anthony was family. Let's work this crime scene like any other.   No, better than any other," Worton said. "Make it your best. He deserves that much. Do not miss anything. Bag that left hand first. He says something is there. Find out what it is. I want every report on my desk by tomorrow. I want my team back in the Precinct conference room as soon as you can get there. I want everyone else out of here, now. Leave him some dignity."

Worton looked once more at Anthony's body, turned on his heel and left the building.

* * *

Ray Pearson, from Behavioral Science, had the floor. He used the projection screen to give visual credence to his team's findings. Copeland, Worton, Morales and Walsh sat across the conference table from him. Each one had a binder to follow.

"Page one is a list of the dates and results of the chess matches between Bobby Fischer and Boris Spassky in Reykjavik, Iceland in 1972. They played 22 games between July 11 and September 1st of that year. Fischer won seven games; Spassky 3. The rest were stalemates, or draws. First, you need to know he is killing people on the dates that coincide with dates when either of the two combatants won matches back in '72. I repeat: only on the days someone won, not the days they played to a draw - at least not so far." The profiler turned to page two.

"The Chess Killer, for want of a better name, killed his first so-called "King" on July 11th, the same date of the first game of the '72 match. Spassky won that match, by the way. Game Two was a forfeit. Fischer did not show up so Spassky won again. That was July 13th and our guy killed again on that same date, this time in Union Square. Game Three, a win this time by Fischer, came three days later on July 16th and once again the killer followed suit, killing this time at The American Academy of Performing Arts. Here it gets interesting because Fischer and Spassky played two days later on July 18th, but "The Chess Killer" does not act. He does not kill on the in-between dates that were draws. He skips to July 20th, the same date as the next victory from 1972. This one is a win by Fischer again. Today is July 20th and today he killed Detective Austin." Preston paused and looked up at the somber room. "Sorry to be blunt."

"Go on." Copeland said.

"Okay, we believe "The Chess Killer" plans to kill ten prominent people, or people whose death will create intense publicity, or both. He plans to kill them on the exact dates that Fischer and Spassky won games during their 1972 World Championship match. The match, itself, or maybe Fischer, seems to be the focal point of his fixation. He has chosen New York City as his chessboard and he plans to kill his victims in the squares that coincide with the squares that held the checkmated kings at the end of each game back in 1972." He paused-then went on.

"Let me expound on that. The folded notes he is leaving have white circles and black circles in each spot or square where they would be found on a chess board set up the same as the wins from '72 and he is doing them in the same order as they happened back then." He is choosing places from each corresponding square, such as Carnegie Hall. Then, he is anointing, or picking, a "King" to checkmate, or in his case, to kill."

Lieutenant Copeland interrupted.

"So let me see if I have this straight. He has killed four people and he plans to kill six more on preset dates, in precise places and we know when and where they will happen?" He asked. Ray Preston put a new chess board of the city on the wall.

	9th Ave.	8th Ave.	7th Ave.	6th Ave.	5th Ave.	4th Ave.	3rd Ave.	2nd Ave.
96th St.								
86th St.								
72nd St.								
57th St.			Carnegie Hall					
42nd St.								
34th St.								
23rd St.					Academy of Preforming Arts			
	9th Ave.	8th Ave.	7th Ave.	6th Ave.	5th Ave.	4th Ave.	3rd Ave.	2nd Ave
14th St.				6th Ave Union Station			3rd Ave. Police Academy	

"Yes, we know the exact dates. But the places are a different story. As you can see, the squares he has chosen are sections of the city that include, at the least, ten city blocks and, at the most, fifteen city blocks. We can easily determine where each king was checkmated and on which date in '72. We already have that information. But finding the exact place he chooses within a corresponding ten block square will be a different story. Not to mention guessing who he is going to target."

"What is his reason? What does he hope to gain?" Nicky Walsh asked.

"Well, that is always our toughest question. There is no way to know exactly what a serial killer is thinking. We can only give our best guess and hope to keep close to him until he makes a mistake. My first guess was that he was fixated on the 1972 "Match" or maybe on Fischer himself. The scary part about this guy is he is leaving clues and contacting the media and calling our detectives and now making it personal with Anthony's death. He doesn't care what we know. He does not think we can beat him. He is treating us like Fischer treated his opponents. Here is why I use the term beat."

He paused and looked directly at Paul Worton who was watching him intently.

"I believe his ultimate goal is to be remembered as the greatest chess player of all time. In fact, more well known than Fischer. The game he has created here is the vehicle that will take him to those heights. He has chosen to play against The New York City Police Department, in particular, the lead detective on the case. That is why he chose to call you, Paul. He wants an opponent. He wants a chess game." he said.

"His warped version of a chess game." Worton said.

Preston spoke again.

"In his mind, if we catch him he loses the match. If he completes the match without being caught, he will have won. And he will definitely be famous." Preston said.

"Yeah, more famous than Bobby Fischer if he kills ten people in New York City and never gets caught." Copeland muttered.

"What's the bottom line going forward Ray?" Worton asked.

Ray Preston checked his notes before he spoke.

"Our target section of the city is between 8th and 9th Avenues and 96th and 106th Streets. Somewhere in that ten block area on July 23rd he is going to kill again."

Paul Worton stood up.

"All right people. We have three days to find the murder scene, the murder victim and the murderer." He said. "Let's get moving."

Tim Copeland stuffed papers back in his file and grabbed Worton's arm as the detective squeezed past him.

"Hey Paul, give me a minute." He said directing the other man into a corner of the room.

"What's up?" Worton asked.

"I'm putting a detail on your family, one at the house and one at Lori's store. I don't like the fact that he has your phone number. I don't like the fact that he is calling you. And I don't want him using you, or them, against us." He watched Worton ponder for a moment and spoke again.

"This is not an option, Paul. I already spoke with Threat Assessment and they agree this threat is credible. He already hit us once. I don't want you or any member of your team doing anything alone until we catch this guy, even if it means staying in the city."

"I'm not arguing, Tim. I really hadn't had time to think in those terms. It can't hurt, but let's keep it low key." Worton said.

"Ok. I'll take care of that end of it. You concentrate on catching this bastard." Copeland said.

Worton watched his boss leave the room. Once again, Tim Copeland was proving why he had moved quickly up the ladder to Commander of a very prestigious detective squad. He would protect his people at all costs, but Worton knew "catching the bastard" would be easier said than done.

* * *

Dusk fell beyond the trees and bushes of the fenced-in back yard. Paul Worton sat on the porch swing hanging from the wooden pergola, above the pressure treated pine deck. The back yard, rich with fragrant flowers and green grass, was surrounded by a flagstone walkway that wound around the porch. Worton took a long pull from the tall glass of rum and coke in his hand, leaned his head back and closed his eyes.

They would bury Anthony in the morning. His peers would wear the dress uniforms. They would form lines, march by his casket and honor his memory. Words would be spoken and flags folded. Bagpipes would play and rifle fire would pierce the air. The mournful sound of taps would drift through the cemetery and tears would flow.

He had been through too many of these gatherings over the last few years. He had buried partners, friends and long time colleagues. He feared that Anthony's funeral would be the worst, maybe because it was the most recent, or maybe because Lori and Jackie were so upset. Lori had almost collapsed when she heard about Anthony. Some of her favorite evenings occurred when Paul brought Anthony home for dinner. He was young and funny and she thought of him as the son she never had. Jackie was almost inconsolable. She crawled on his lap and cried on his shoulder for close to an hour. The last time she did that she was a child and he could not remember the reason for her tears. She adored Anthony. He joked that Jackie was his best girl and he would wait until she was old enough to settle down and get married. She would always hit him and protest, but she could never hide her smile.

Worton drained the last of his drink. He had wanted Anthony on his team and pulled strings to make it happen. Now Anthony was gone.

His phone rang.

"Worton here."

"Paul? Ray Pearson here. You said you wanted to be kept up to date. We have come up with a few things and I didn't know if you wanted to hear it now or wait until you get to the station tomorrow".

"Let's hear it."

"Well, some of this stuff is about Anthony, Paul."

"I said let's hear it, Ray."

"Ok. The weapon was a long, thin blade. He was stabbed twice. Once from behind, which severed a portion of his spinal column leaving him at least partially paralyzed from the waist down. I think this blow came first. The second and fatal wound was from the front, ripping straight through his spleen, causing massive blood loss. The M. E. says the placement of both wounds was perfect. He believes the killer must have had some kind of training in anatomy. Medical school, or work in a hospital or a mortuary, something along those lines."

"What was in his hand Ray?" Paul interrupted.

"I was getting to that Paul. He knew he was dying. His left thumb and forefinger were pressed together. Between them we found short, blonde human hairs. We are awaiting DNA. If he is in the system, we will know tonight."

"How about our site search, any luck yet?"

"Not yet. Ten blocks is an awfully big area to search, even if we knew exactly what to look for. Who knows what he is thinking? It's like finding a needle in a haystack." Pearson answered.

"Ok. Stay on it. I have a copy of the map here and will continue to try to find a clue myself. I will be at the station after the service."

He hung up and leaned forward, elbows on knees. He watched the sun set beyond the Crape Myrtles that lined the picket fence bordering the yard. The telephone in his hand rang a second time. He did not recognize the number and no name appeared on his caller ID.

Worton knew who it was.

Anger flooded his mind but he forced it back as the phone rang again.

"I wondered when I would hear from you again." He said, keeping his voice as controlled as possible.

"First, let me give my condolences for your loss. It was not my original plan to include Officer Austin in our game. I hope you believe me, Detective. It was just a coincidence that happened to come along. When it did, I could not resist. I knew it would get your attention." The voice said.

"It does not matter whether I believe you or not. What matters is what happens next. What matters is which unassuming, innocent victim you plan to execute next." Worton spoke in a complete monotone trying to keep all emotion out of his voice.

"Maybe I am done Detective. Maybe I am satisfied with my mission."

"No. My experience tells me that psychopathic killers are just like child molesters. They only stop if they are caught and put away." Worton said.

There was an edge to the voice when it spoke, an emotion that Worton could clearly hear.

"I am no child molester, Detective. You insult my intelligence. Don't make the mistake of lumping me in with some degenerate criminal." He whispered.

"Oh no? You have killed four people at random and left some kind of crazy clue on each one suggesting some sort of vicious board game, but you are totally sane." Worton said sarcastically.

After a long pause, the voice spoke in its original tone.

"I believe you have made more progress than you are letting on Detective. At least I hope so, or this game will be no challenge at all. Good night, Detective. You have a long, emotional day ahead of you. My condolences again."

The line went dead.

* * *

GAME 5

July 23rd

*"Even a person who doesn't know chess can watch it as a sporting event.
There is an ebb and flow in terms of aggression, attack and defense."*

Shelby Lyman

New York City still serves as the true melting pot of the world. The City is made up of every faction, of every ethnic group, on the face of the earth. The diversity of each group stems from geographical, to religious, to culture, to financial status.

White Anglo Saxons can be found everywhere, from the boardrooms of Wall Street to the panhandlers of Central Park. African Americans range from Presidential nominees, to bank executives, to housewives, to street punks. The Jewish community is a combination of different religious sects, from small radical thinking groups such as The Neturi Kanta non Zionist group, to the more common divisions of synagogues such as Orthodox, Conservatives and Reform Judaism. The Asian community splits first by origin, Japanese, Chinese, Vietnamese, and so on, before splitting again from those steeped in old family traditions, all the way to those who have whole heartedly embraced the American way of life.

Spanish speaking Americans hail from every corner of the world including Spain, South America, Central America, Puerto

Rico and beyond. Every faction of this group can be found in the upper east corner of the city between 1ˢᵗ and 4ᵗʰ Avenue and 96ᵗʰ and 125ᵗʰ Street, in an area called Spanish Harlem.

Spanish Harlem started as a Dutch German settlement in the late 1600's, soon to be followed by Irish, Italian and Russian Jewish immigrants. Sicilians and Southern Italians dominated East Harlem, which became the hub of Italian Americans in Manhattan. The term Spanish Harlem arose soon after WWI, with a large influx of Puerto Ricans into the western portion of what was then known as Italian Harlem. Slowly, the Italians moved out as more and more Latinos moved in after WW II, and the entire area soon became known as Spanish Harlem.

During the 60's and 70's, Spanish Harlem struggled with drugs, race riots, poverty and corruption, worse than any other part of the city. But today, the area known as "El Barrio" which remains predominantly Latino has seen resurgence, along with the marked improvement of all of Manhattan. Small pockets of Chinese, Korean, Blacks and Whites have moved back into the area to set up shop. But as the saying goes, "the more things change the more they stay the same." The area remains Spanish Harlem for a reason.

Angel Jesus Vargas sat on the end of the bleachers inside the chain link fence. The ball field was a part of a park complex located between 96ᵗʰ and 97ᵗʰ Street, just east of 2ⁿᵈ Avenue, at the bottom end of Spanish Harlem. The park remained the home base for *Los Tainos*, the most respected and feared gang in New York City. The Puerto Rican-based group was almost fifty years old, having grown out of the poverty and desperation that permeated the barrio for four decades. At its inception, the name *Los Tainos* stood for nothing more than poor Spanish speaking young men trying to survive any way possible. They knew it was an ancestral name from days gone by, before their forefathers moved to the island of Puerto Rico. But to them, it was a name to distinguish themselves from other Spanish speaking gangs springing up throughout the city.

Vargas was thirty years old, older than any other gang leader in Manhattan. He was grandfathered in to *Los Tainos* at the age of eight as the younger brother of a *Taino* lieutenant. He dropped out of school and never looked back. By his twentieth birthday, he was the unquestioned leader of the most powerful gang the City of New York had ever seen. Under his reign, *Los Tainos* grudgingly gained respect, not just from other gangs but from business leaders, residents of Spanish Harlem and, most importantly, from the cops themselves. *Los Tainos* sold and distributed drugs all over the city, more than any other individual or group. But Angel Vargas had rules. Rules his people lived by, or they did not work for him. If they did work for him and they broke his rules, they paid dearly, sometimes with their lives.

No drugs were sold to children or near any school, especially within Spanish Harlem. All school age children of gang members must go to school. No child was allowed to join the gang until he finished high school. Any gang member who had a run in with the cops would answer to Vargas himself. All elderly relatives must be treated with respect and taken care of by their children, or by the resources of the gang. No murderer, child molester or rapist would be hidden by *Los Tainos*. To Angel Jesus Vargas, *Los Tainos* was a business and it would be run as cleanly and efficiently as possible. He had no illusions about the substances he sold or what they could do to people, but in his mind, adults had many ways to ruin their lives and someone would always profit from it, why not *Los Tainos*?

He had changed the landscape even more for his immediate followers. The use of the products they sold to the public was forbidden. He was a part time user himself as a young man and understood not everyone could resist, but to be close to Angel or his family there were no exceptions. He kept six men close to him. They grew up with him as young *Tainos* and knew no other life. He knew they were devoted to him and that they would not understand, one day, when he was gone. Gone with no warning. No goodbye. No forwarding address. Just gone.

Angel Jesus Vargas had a long term plan. He was five years away from that plan. At the age of thirty five he, his wife Maria, their daughter Juanita and their son Miguel would disappear. Just like that. For ten years he had been stocking money away in a bank account in New Mexico. Only Maria knew the plan. They had one goal: to keep his family clean and safe. To get out rich and free to do as they please for the rest of their lives. *Los Tainos* was a means to an end and his closest friends would not understand. When he was gone, they would turn on each other to claim his empire.

Good luck to them, he thought, as he gazed out across the painted green playing field at Mark Brothers Playground. The fenced in park and playground served as a daytime play area for the families and friends of *Los Tainos*. The enclosed artificial turf soccer and baseball fields, basketball courts and restrooms served as retail counters for the business transactions of *Los Tainos* that took place from dusk till dawn, seven days a week. No sales in daylight. No sales in the open. No sales that would put any of his law enforcement "friends" in jeopardy. He took care of his "friends" and his protection was complete.

Angel came to the park for an afternoon coed softball game. He played a couple of innings here and there, jumping in where he saw fit. He watched for a couple more innings then headed to the sandbox/jungle gym area just outside the fence by the restrooms. Juanita, his seven year old, and her friends were having a ball on the jungle gym and swings. Miguel, the five year old, was standing by the sandbox. Angel grinned as he sat across the picnic table from Maria. Miguel would spend hours running his bright red remote controlled truck through the sandbox as though nothing else in the world existed. Angel would sit with Maria, have a few beers and talk for awhile.

Ramon Ortiz and Manuel Cruz were the two bodyguards with Angel Vargas this day. When he played softball, they sat on the bench. When he sat at the table to watch his children and drink beer, they sat a few tables away drinking beer and watching him. Vargas cut his conversation with Maria short.

"Ramon! Manny! Why so many cops today? They seem to be everywhere."

On the morning ride in, he noticed patrol cars on almost every street. Plain clothes detectives at different buildings and businesses, and now a build-up of cops in front of The Metro Hospital located up 2nd Avenue across 97th street.

"Find someone we know and get an answer." Vargas said. He was more curious than worried, but always better to be safe. As Ramon ambled up the street to carry out the order, Manuel, now alert and watchful, moved closer to his boss. His focus was always Angel Vargas first, Maria and the children second and everyone else third.

* * *

Every available officer from every division of New York City's finest was busy scowering Spanish Harlem. It was an exhausting and almost impossible job. They did not know who they were looking for or where to look. But they were relentless. They checked every possible person who could be considered a "king". Predominate citizens and well-known places were interviewed and checked. Business leaders, celebrities, people with the last name King, corporations and famous landmarks. All of which led Paul Worton and his team to the entrance of The Metro Hospital Center, just north of 96th Street. To Worton, it was the only place that stood out between 96th and 106th Streets.

"Ok. Make sure you check for anyone named King. Doctors, nurses or patients, I don't care how stupid it seems. The head of every department in the hospital has to be protected, whether they like it or not." Worton said to the investigators huddled around him. "I know we could be way off base here, but it's our best guess. I really don't know what more we can do."

The loud screeching of tires down the avenue and across 96th Street ripped through Worton's jagged nerves.

* * *

Angel Vargas was not the only one who noticed the law enforcement build up in Spanish Harlem. Michael Mueller slipped back in the shadows of the stone restroom and smiled. He wore faded jeans and a skin tight white tank top. His long, jet black hair was pulled back in a shoulder length ponytail. A lone silver cross hung from his right ear, while ancestral Latino tattoos lined both tanned muscular arms. He could be mistaken for a member of any Latino gang by an outsider, but within Spanish Harlem he would stand out as a newcomer in an instant. He would not be around long enough for that to matter.

He knew why the cops were in Spanish Harlem and he was thrilled. They had to know today was the date for game five. It meant someone had figured out the clues. They must know the dates for all the games if they knew this one. It meant Paul Worton had been less than honest with him. He could not have been happier. The game was on!

He stepped out of the back entrance to the restroom and made his way up 3rd Avenue to the corner of 96th Street, and headed down the street on foot. He slowed his walk, waiting for the next on-coming vehicle to approach a certain spot. He then pressed a button on a small transmitter in his pocket.

* * *

Little Miguel Vargas could not understand why his bright red truck drove out of the sandbox and away from him. He pressed the buttons to stop his truck the way his daddy had shown him.

The truck did not stop. It kept moving away from him. Miguel ran after his favorite toy, yelling at the top of his lungs.

"Stop! Come back! Stop!"

Angel Vargas was in mid-sentence talking to Maria when he heard his son's shout. His eyes turned and he reacted before it all registered in his mind. Miguel was chasing his truck which was passing between two parked cars, while a pickup truck moving at about thirty miles an hour closed on the opening. Angel was yelling his son's name as he clambered over the table top. He knew he was too late. Maria was screaming and all other activity in and around the park stopped as Miguel disappeared between the two cars as fast as his little feet could carry him. Angel's stomach churned as he waited to hear the sickening thud.

It never came.

A body crashed on the hood of the white Impala sedan and an arm grabbed Miguel by the back of his shirt flinging him backwards. The man's momentum caused him to bounce off the hood and slam into the right rear panel of the truck, which crushed the mini red toy and skidded to a stop thirty feet away. Bedlam ensued. The truck driver jumped from his truck apologizing to everyone who would listen. He swore that he never saw the boy or the toy truck. *Los Tainos* gang members quickly grabbed and held the man. Maria Vargas engulfed her son in her arms, checking every inch of her son's body for injury. She was crying, scolding and hugging him at the same time, causing her frightened son to cry along with her. Juanita and her friends cried because her mom and brother were crying. The *Los Tainos* wives and children quickly gathered for support, while gang members formed a protective ring around the entire group.

The young Columbian slowly rose from the pavement and staggered, until one of the gathering crowd grabbed his arm to support him. Michael did not need help. He had tucked his shoulder and hit the truck with exactly the force he intended. He spoke in Spanish and professed to be fine. He was surrounded now, and pretended to be a bit intimidated. He was telling everyone he did not need medical attention, when the crowd parted and Angel Vargas stood in front of him.

"You are the man who saved my son's life?" he asked.

The young hero answered in Spanish, with a perfect Columbian accent.

"I am sorry. My English is not good," he said.

"You saved my son's life." Vargas said, this time in Spanish.

"Ah! He is so small. He did not see the truck. What could I do? I had no choice but to act."

Angel Vargas caught the man in a bear hug

"You saved my only son's life. I do not know how to thank you but, be assured, I am indebted to you. I will never forget this."

"No! No! You owe me nothing. He is only a boy. Anyone would do the same," the man protested, pushing back away from Vargas.

"Who are you strange savior? I do not know you. Do you have family here in the Barrio?" Vargas asked.

"My name is Luis Martinez. I am from Columbia. We are new here."

The crowd was big now. Police cars were arriving and cops were making their way through the throng of onlookers. The young man looked anxiously over Vargas's shoulder.

"I must go now," he whispered to Vargas. "I cannot speak to the police."

Vargas knew instantly the man's problem. He had no green card.

"You are an illegal?" Vargas asked.

"Yes! Yes! Please I must go," he said, feigning fear and pulling away. Vargas acted quickly.

"Manuel, take my new friend away. Keep him hidden. I will take care of this Luis. Do not worry," he said. Vargas then pushed out through the crowd towards the arriving police cars as Manuel whisked his boss's new friend away from the accident scene and back towards the picnic tables.

The King's Gambit

Angel Vargas went to work as only a leader with complete confidence can do. He spoke to the crowd, which quickly dispersed. He then met with the police officers at the scene and the truck driver. In a matter of minutes, the street was clear, the softball game had resumed and he was walking back to the picnic table where Manuel had taken Luis Martinez. Maria sat across from the two men, clinging tightly to her son. Juanita sat next to her, wiping her eyes and hugging her mother's leg. Vargas spoke to his wife.

"Maria, this is the man who saved Miguel."

She did not release her hold on Miguel, but made her way around the table to hug the young man and kiss his forehead. Vargas instructed Manuel to take his family home and to wait there for his return. When they were alone at the table, with only a few *Los Tainos* gang members standing guard around the park's perimeter, Vargas turned his attention to the man he knew as Luis Martinez. The two men talked for over an hour. The man told a story of a poor upbringing in Columbia. How he brought his family to the United States to make a better life. He could not find steady work and his family of six lived in a one bedroom apartment barely surviving. Angel Vargas told the man his worries were over. His family was now part of the Vargas family and would remain under his protection. He would have a job, and his family would never be hungry again.

The man pretended to be shocked by the generosity. He protested for a while that he deserved no reward. That he only did what any man would do. Vargas would hear none of it. Luis Martinez would return to the park that very night to be indoctrinated into the *Los Tainos* way of life. The two men parted company after hugs and handshakes, profusely thanking each other and promising to be friends forever.

The newest *Los Tainos* recruit left the park promising to come back that night, after dark, and meet Angel Vargas at the same picnic table. But he knew they would be meeting much sooner. When he reached the end of 96th Street, he doubled back and approached the stone bathroom from the other side of the jungle gym area. He slipped in the backside entrance and entered the men's room. He jimmied the lock to the janitor's closet, stepped inside and waited.

Angel Vargas met with all his lieutenants, and reviewed that night's game plan.

Who would be used to deliver? Who would stand watch? Who was on duty in the area for police protection? When and where would all drops be made? When he was satisfied with the answers he got up to leave, giving his men the signal to disperse and return for work later. Vargas spoke to Ramon.

"I need to take a squirt. Tell Tito to get the car."

Angel Jesus Vargas headed for the stone restroom like he did every time he left the park for his ride home. Angel had one weakness. When he drank beer, he had to take a leak.

* * *

By the time the crowd started to gather around the fallen man and the truck, Paul Worton had already dispatched Jose Morales, and two patrol officers, to check out the commotion. He was sure it was just one of the hundreds of minor accidents that permeate the city every day and, so far, his killer had acted in secret, never putting himself in jeopardy of being caught. But Worton was taking no chances. Today, every possibility would be investigated, including fender benders.

Twenty minutes later, Worton was going over a hospital personnel list, and a list of all patients currently staying in the medical center. He looked up as Morales returned.

"Anything?" He asked.

"No not really. Kid was chasing his toy car into the street and some passerby pulled the kid back just in time. No fault to the driver. He couldn't see the kid or the truck because it went between cars, and the guy wasn't speeding. I left it to the patrol guys. Nothing that helps us." Morales said.

"Great. Okay, let's get into this list. We have three possibilities. Two are here, one is not. We need to find where this Dr. Amanda King lives and where she is right now. We will check out the other two. The first one is a stretch. A guy named Michael Royal. He is a cook working in the cafeteria. Our guy is killing "Kings", maybe Royal is the connection. I don't know, but I'm not taking any chances. The other guy is Joshua Blomberg." Worton said.

"Blomberg the author? He must have ten bestsellers now. I love his stuff. He could definitely be our target." Morales said.

"Yeah, it's the same Blomberg. Already got people posted in his room and outside of his door. We have people in the cafeteria with this Royal guy. Let's go talk to both of them." Worton said. As the two men walked into the hospital, Worton flipped open his cell phone and called Tim Copeland.

"Tim. Worton here. We are at The Metro Medical Center over by 96th Street, checking leads in the hospital. The best we have is Joshua Blomberg, the author. He is a patient here. Some minor procedure, only supposed to be here one night. Yeah, he is being guarded and we are going to talk to him now. Nothing from the rest of the canvas? Okay, I'll keep you up to date and I'll be in your office some time after midnight. See you then." Worton hung up as they reached the elevators.

Forty-five minutes later they were back at Worton's car, in front of the building. Their interview with Blomberg and his wife had garnered no new information. The two detectives were discussing their next move when two patrol officers approached.

"Sorry to interrupt, detective. I thought you would want a report on the commotion down the street, so we hung around," the first officer said. Morales turned to the two officers who had responded with him earlier.

"Just routine right?" he asked.

"Yeah, nothing going on over there. The *Los Tainos* gang hangs out at that park a lot, and it seems their leader Angel Vargas's son ran out in front of an oncoming vehicle, and his dad pulled him back just in time. The guy in the truck wasn't drinking or speeding and Vargas said the kid was fine," the first officer said. Worton was half listening when he looked up from the papers in his hand.

"I thought some passerby saved the kid?" he said.

"That's what a guy who saw the whole thing told me." Detective Morales said. "He was in a car coming the other way and saw a guy walking along, jump on the hood of a car, roll off and slam into the truck. He said he didn't realize the kid was there until he ran over to see if the guy was okay."

"I don't know, Detective. Vargas told us he grabbed his kid and everyone was fine. He never mentioned any other guy," the officer said.

Paul Worton felt the hair crawl on his neck.

"Jose, get Walsh and anyone else who does not have a specific duty here. Leave everyone else in place. You two come with me," he said pointing to the uniformed officers.

* * *

Angel Vargas had to piss like a racehorse. He usually had to go every half hour after drinking beer, but with Miguel's close call he never noticed the need. He stood at the middle urinal and unzipped, leaning in and resting his head against the wall. The relief he felt was more than the relief of his bladder. Miguel had almost died. He could not believe his negligence. Thank God for Luis Martinez. Only divine providence could have brought such a man along just at the right time. Tears welled in his eyes.

"Thank you Jesus," he whispered.

A sound behind him made him flinch. He knew he was as vulnerable as a man could be. Slowly, he turned his head as he freed his hands to act if necessary.

Paul Worton stood in the men's room doorway.

"Do you like to watch men urinate, *Maricon*?" He sneered at Worton.

"I don't speak a lot of Spanish so I'm not sure what I was just called, but I'm pretty sure it wasn't a compliment," Worton said as he surveyed the room. "To answer your question no, in fact, I'm pretty sure I don't want to be in any room with you, but circumstances have brought us together."

Vargas gave himself a last shake and zipped his fly, stepping away from the urinal. Worton's eyes never left the wary drug dealer as he opened the doors to all three stalls in the room, and tried the doorknob on the janitor's closet. He did so making a complete tour of the room, ending up at the opposite end from the door he used to enter the room.

Michael Mueller stood on the other side of the closet door holding the door handle tightly shut as he touched his ear to the door and listened to his opponent, and his next victim. Finally, Vargas spoke.

"What do you want here?"

"Where is the man who saved your boy's life?" Worton asked.

"No such man exists. I pulled my boy to safety."

"Okay. Let me tell you a story Angel. I am Homicide Detective Paul Worton. I don't care about you, your gang or your son although I am happy the boy was not hurt today. I am investigating four murders in the city over the last two weeks. Maybe you read or watch the news. First Carnegie Hall, then Union Square, then a professor on 26th and Madison and finally, one of my detectives. If we are right, the next murder is going to take place in Spanish Harlem today." Worton said.

Vargas looked confused, but stuck to his story.

"All of that has nothing to do with me or my son." Worton stepped closer to Angel Vargas.

"If I am right, it has everything to do with you. The man who saved your son is my killer. He set you up to get close to you. He is here to make you his fifth victim," Worton said.

"You are crazy. Why me and how could he know Miguel would run to the street right at that moment? It is impossible." Vargas protested.

Worton reached a rubber-gloved hand in his pocket and pulled out a small clear evidence bag. Inside the bag was a small black object that fit in the palm of his hand. It was rectangle in shape, and had a small red button on one end.

"We found this in the street next to the skid marks on the road. It's a remote control device. Your savior must have dropped it when he hit the truck or the ground. When you press this button, what is left of your kid's truck kinda creeps along on the two wheels that are still attached. He sent the boy's toy into the street. He knew Miguel would chase the truck and he knew if he saved the boy you would trust him." Worton said.

Angel Vargas stared at the object. He could not believe his ears. His stomach turned and he seethed with anger.

"I will kill him with my bare hands. What if he was not in time? He played games with my son's life. He made a fool of me. He lied to me. I vowed to be friends for life, to take care of him and his family. I will kill him," he screamed.

"Angel, when is he coming back? When are you meeting him?"

"This is my concern. I will deal with this bastard." Vargas spit the words with venom.

Worton was suddenly in the gang lord's face.

"You listen and you listen good. The six guys outside protecting you are in cuffs right now. You will be in a lockup until this night is over. After that, he will not come after you. It is a game to him and it has to happen today. You are a random victim. Maybe he wants to create a gang war or a racial upheaval. He is looking for as much press as possible. If you tell me where and when you are supposed to meet him, we have a chance to catch him. If not, you go to jail for your own safety and he goes free. Your choice."

Vargas stared at Worton for a moment. He knew men and he knew this cop would not give in.

"Okay. He is to meet me here tonight at seven o'clock. But why not just let me kill him? That way I am happy and your case is solved, and we save the taxpayers some money."

"No, that won't work, Angel, because you are not good enough. He would kill you and I would have five murders to solve." Worton said. "Let's go."

* * *

Michael Mueller stood in the dark behind the janitor's door. He was turning the knob to carry out his plan when he heard Paul Worton confront Vargas. He was shocked to say the least. He quickly calmed his nerves and held the door tightly shut. He felt Worton try the knob and made sure it did not turn. His surprise grew as he listened to the two men talk. He reached quickly in his pocket, and swore silently to himself, when Worton spoke of the black object he found in the street. A major blunder. Many championship games were lost at just such a moment. But, again, he calmed himself. Just as many great champions, including the great Bobby Fischer, had pulled themselves back from such mistakes and gone on to win matches, he could do the same. He listened to Worton's every word. He was impressed. The man had fooled him. The detective had lulled him into a false sense of security. The police were far ahead of where he imagined them to be. He listened until the two men were gone. He slid to the floor, sat and waited. He knew it would be a long wait. It was close to 2:00 a.m. before he slipped out of the closet and headed back towards Central Park. He was stiff and hungry, but he felt invigorated more than any time since the game had started. He would have to concede game five. Like all great champions, he hated to lose. Losing the remote was a blunder and his opponent took advantage. The good news was that his opponent could play the game.

He smiled as he walked. The real challenges lay ahead. He could not wait for game six.

* * *

Detective Squad Commander Tim Copeland's office was not that big. A desk, three chairs, a filing cabinet, an overhead TV monitor and coffee pot. The walls were lined with pictures and citations that marked the detective's thirty year career. The most important item in the room, as far as Copeland was concerned, was the coffee pot. He poured his eighth cup of the day and returned to his desk. Copeland swallowed half of the hot black liquid and placed the cup on the desk. He leaned back in his chair and ran both hands through his hair before clasping them behind his head. He spoke to the three police officers in front of him.

"Okay, it looks like we prevented a murder last night. That is assuming all our calculations are correct. That's the good news. The bad news is that we had this guy lying in the street right at our feet and couldn't nab him. So what happened? Give me something here Paul," Copeland said.

Paul Worton sat in the middle chair between Detective Jose Morales and Officer Nicky Walsh.

"Well, I think we confirmed last night that our calculations are correct. Unless we stumbled onto the most bizarre coincidence in history, our guy planned to kill Angel Jesus Vargas, the head of Spanish Harlem's most notorious gang. Angel Vargas was to be "king" for a day in our killer's mind. Our killer staged a near accident where he managed to save the life of the kid to get close to Vargas. He was disguised as a Latino immigrant and Vargas, who was obviously very grateful, promised to take care of him and his family. He was to return around seven to, I guess, join the gang. But his intent was to kill Vargas," Worton paused to look at his notes. "We got conflicting reports on the near accident and checked a little closer. We got lucky. It seems our killer dropped the remote he used to entice the boy into the street, which led us to Vargas. I'm pretty confident he backed off when he saw the police presence and realized we were on to him. We put Vargas under protective custody until tomorrow, using the theory he will only kill on the same dates as the Fischer/Spassky matches."

"Okay. I need to get a handle on where this goes from here. This has become a very hot, media driven case. I need something I can sell to the Chief of Detectives. Andy Wiley, the kid from Channel 4 News, is not talking about where he got his information. The station had its lawyers here in a flash and we had to release him. But he may talk yet, when he is facing a court injunction and a stint in jail," Copeland said. Pausing for a second, he looked directly at Paul Worton. "You know, originally I was convinced that Wiley had a mole inside the department, but now I am not so sure. What if our killer is talking to the press just like he is with you?"

Worton did not answer for a few minutes. He sat staring at Tim Copeland, mulling the thought over in his mind.

"You're right. Of course you're right. He wants an audience. What better way to make his time in the spotlight memorable than going directly to the media," Worton said. "I hear he just signed with *The Daily News* to write a daily column. His first assignment, of course, is this case. The question is, are we better off with Wiley in jail, or maybe trying to use him?"

"Let's get him back in here. With his lawyers if that is the only way. Feel him out. Try to make a deal with him, keeping the threat of jail time hanging over his head," Copeland instructed. "Maybe, just maybe, he has some deep seeded longing to help the police and do what is best for society. If not, maybe we just lock his ass up. Anyway, have Morales and Walsh pick him up. How are we with the next date and location?"

"Four days away on the 27th between 4th and 5th Avenues somewhere from 86th Street to 96th Street. The Guggenheim Museum is on 92nd Street and 5th Avenue. It has to be the place. High profile, right up his ally. A game six win in one of the most popular tourist attractions in the city. What more could he want?" Worton said.

"Do we have a potential target?" Copeland asked.

"Well, Sir," Nicky Walsh said. "Believe it or not, it seems on their respective birthdays, every employee at The Guggenheim wears a paper crown all day long at work. The thinking is our guy would love the irony."

"That is nice to know Officer Walsh, but it seems way too obvious. If it is obvious to me it will certainly be obvious to him. Why would he put himself in such jeopardy?" Copeland asked.

"'Boss, we have a meeting scheduled as soon as we leave here with Robert Nugent and Victor Menchenko. Let me bring them here now. I think they may give us some insight to what this guy is thinking." Worton said.

Copeland stood and refilled his cup.

"Do it," he said.

Fifteen minutes later, Worton addressed the assembled group.

"This is a highly intelligent guy we're dealing with. We have to assume he didn't kill on the 23rd because we were there. That means he knows we have the dates and approximate locations of the last five murders. If we are correct about the Guggenheim, he will assume we will be there. If he is targeting the employees wearing crowns on that day, he will know we are going to protect them. He knows we will be there or close by each time. It will not stop him. But it will make him even more wary," Worton said.

"Then I have to ask again, why would he put himself in harm's way?" Copeland asked.

Robert Nugent coughed and tentatively raised his hand as he spoke.

"I'm sorry for interrupting, is it okay Paul?" He asked.

"Sure Nuge. What have you got?" Worton said.

"I know it is hard to do, but you have to understand that he is playing chess. Well, he thinks he is even though we know he is killing people. But he is playing against you as if you are a chess opponent. In chess, most players know something about the other player's next move. I think Mr. Menchenko could express it better than I can. He has played chess at the highest level in the world," Nuge said.

All eyes turned to the grandmaster. The white haired gentleman sat staring for a moment at his hands which were clasped in front of him. He took a deep breath and stood. He shook his head and then spoke with great passion in his voice.

"I have loved the game of chess my whole life. As a boy, before my parents brought us to this great country, I played chess. It is my only memory of the old country. I have played, competed and watched the greats from all over the world. It has been my whole life, and now a madman is using the game I love as an excuse to kill people."

"Whatever we learn from you might stop him, Mr. Menchencko," Tim Copeland said.

"You are, of course, correct," the older man said. He stuck both thumbs in the small pockets of his vest and started to pace in front of his audience.

"In a game of chess, especially one played by elite players, each player knows every possible move his opponent might make. Opening moves, offensive and defensive strategies, all have names known to all great players. These strategies and moves bear the names of the great chess champions of the past, and evoke well known counter moves. If he is a great player, he will expect you to recognize his moves and he will expect counter moves." Victor Menchenko was in his element, teaching the game of chess. He concentrated on every word as he stalked back and forth. "You must remember, in this case you are dealing with a match, not a game. A match is a series of games leading to an eventual champion. In a match, you try to win every game but you know you will, in all likelihood, play games within a match to a draw. He will consider yesterday's game as a draw not a failure, and if he cannot get to his intended victim at the Guggenheim, he will consider that a draw and move on to his next game. His goal is to win the match. To what end I cannot answer, but that is his goal."

"So it is possible that he will go to The Guggenheim on the 27th, but back away again if he thinks we are on to him?" Worton asked.

"I have never dealt with a psychopath, but as a chess player he will certainly be there to play the game. Remember, every great chess player sacrifices pieces during a game to improve his chances of winning. If the means justifies the end, every piece on the board is expendable including the queen, which is by far the most lethal weapon on the board. If he is as smart as you think he is, and an exceptional chess player, he will have strategies mapped out to counter any attack on him. And, if he has to give ground to win, he will do so."

"Detective, he is no longer trying to get our attention and, judging by the fact that he has called you directly, I believe he has dismissed everyone else from his game. In his mind, he is playing this game against you."

Tim Copeland's cell phone broke the silence in the room.

"Copeland here. Really! Fax it over to my office and get a complete run down on this guy. I want to know everything from the day he was born until now. Up to and including where he gets his hair done. Got it? Thanks. Good work," he said before hanging up.

"That was the Crime Lab. First, they can confirm that our boy planned to kill Vargas last night. He was in the janitor's closet in the men's room at some point. Crime Scene found one of his folded paper chess boards just inside the door. So he was definitely there. On another front, we got lucky. DNA from the hair we found in Anthony's hand was not in the system, but they got a partial print off the remote he dropped in the street, and they got a match. They are sending the info over by fax. The man's name is Michael Mueller.

"Who?" Victor Menchenko asked.

The King's Gambit

"Michael Mueller." Tim Copeland said as all eyes turned to the ashen-faced grandmaster.

"I think I know this name," he whispered.

* * *

Michael Mueller sat at the desk in the small hidden room of his townhouse and slowly, carefully, peeled the skin tight flesh colored gloves from his hands and hung them on a hook at the side of the desk.

* * *

Lori Worton was worried about her husband. She was a cop's wife, so she worried every day. Maybe more than most, because she had been on the job and seen first-hand what the job could do to a person, both physically and mentally. September 11th was an exception as far as loss of life was concerned for a single day, but the threat of losing a loved one was real every day he or she walked out the door. Now he was dealing with a serial killer, and the killer had called Paul directly. She sat alone on the top step of the bleachers and yelled a word of encouragement to her daughter.

Jacquelyn Worton's fingers twisted and turned the front of her navy blue softball jersey. It was a habit her teammates were accustomed to, but opponents had come to fear. Jackie took her usual windmill windup, slapped her glove on her thigh and snapped a blistering fastball over the outside corner for a called third strike. Lori Worton smiled. It was inevitable: whenever Jackie needed a little extra zip on the ball, you could hear that slap of leather on her leg clear out to the parking lot. She also knew that Jackie was not just twisting the front of her jersey. Under her game shirt Jackie always wore a short sleeve Under Armour T-shirt, and under her tee, on a long silver chain, she wore her dad's high school championship ring. At crunch time, she touched the ring for good luck and went about her business.

She could not believe Anthony had been dead a week. Murdered the same night she and Paul made love in their friend's apartment. The sicko called Paul at home the night before the funeral, and she had not seen Paul since he left the cemetery the next day.

Lori shaded her eyes and looked down the left field line beyond the outfield fence. The olive green, unmarked SUV had been parked on a side street behind her home for more than a week. Now the vehicle, with its tinted windows, blended in with all of the other cars in the second row of the gravel parking lot. Paul insisted they were in no danger and she pretty much agreed that they were not targets. Still, each day when she went to work she felt better knowing someone was watching out for her daughter.

"Atta girl, Jackie!" she yelled, as the fourteen year old struck out her third batter of the inning and tenth of the game.

Jackie grinned up at her mom as she ran to the dugout. Lori thought of how disappointed she had looked when she found out her father could not make the game. He loved to watch her play. He spent an entire weekend constructing a mound and home plate to the exact pitching dimensions for girls fast pitch softball. They spent countless hours in the backyard. Her pitching and him catching and coaching. His football ring was his prized possession. He had never taken it off from the day it was presented to him. He scored the go-ahead touchdown in the State Championship game on a quarterback-keeper from forty-five yards out. He hit the hole, cut back and out ran the opposition to an undefeated senior season. Six days later, Paul Worton's dad died of cancer. He wore the ring to honor his teammates and he wore the ring to honor his dad. Then one day, he gave the ring to Jackie. He told her he would not always be able to make her games in person, but as long as she had the ring her dad would always be with her. They were so close, Lori thought.

"Please keep him safe," she breathed in quiet prayer.

Jackie Worton ripped a pitch down the third base line and sprinted towards first base.

"Way to go baby!" Lori yelled.

* * *

Paul Worton sat in the backseat and read the newly printed dossier on Michael Muller out loud.

"He was born June 28th, 1980 at South Hampton Hospital, to Jefferson and Marion Mueller of Sag Harbor. Jefferson Mueller was born into money and quadrupled his wealth with good investments and a very lucrative art business. Marion Mueller did not then and still does not work. She is very busy in local events and activities. She gets her money from a trust set up by her husband before he died in 1995. He died of prostate cancer. It seems she turned the trust fund over to her son when he turned twenty-one, seven years ago. Bank records are being subpoenaed as we speak. If Copeland finds anything that could help us he'll fax it to the Suffolk County P.D. Mueller was privately tutored from the first through the fifth grade, then he went to Sag Harbor Elementary School and then on to Sag Harbor High School. He graduated at the top of his class and was accepted early to Harvard, where he graduated Magna Cum Laude in only three years." Worton took a deep breath.

"Great, he is even smarter than we thought. Two years at Rutgers School of Medicine and here is where it gets weird. Seems he never did his residency in Chicago. He spent the next five years as a stage hand in a theater in Montana, a ski instructor and personnel trainer in Colorado and a bounty hunter in California. He had to register for a license out there to be a bounty hunter and that is where the F.B.I. got his prints. Right now, he is employed as a blackjack dealer at The Mohegan Sun Casino in Connecticut. His family has owned the same house in Sag Harbor for almost forty years and, as far as this report states, he is still living there with his mother," Worton said. "Anyone have any thoughts?"

"Well, he is brilliant and the medical school background would explain his knowledge of the human body and how to attack it." Morales said from the front driver's seat.

"And working as a bounty hunter explains his knowledge of police work and weapons. He spent two years in a theater. Doing what I wonder?" Nicky Walsh added.

"We will know soon enough. We have people checking every place we can put him over the last ten years. They are conducting interviews right now. We should have that information this afternoon." Worton said.

"One thing we know for sure is that he has a chess history." Nicky Walsh said.

Before they left the 18th precinct, Victor Menchencko related the story of a young boy and his desperate father, trying to make the boy something he was not. He told of countless teaching sessions, games and tournaments all leading to one conclusion. The boy was just not good enough at the game of chess. The boy's father was crushed by the news and the boy was crying as they left his studio. He never heard from them again, but he had told them the truth. Victor Menchencko was sure this could not be the same boy.

It was looking more and more like the great chess master was wrong. It seemed Michael Mueller was exactly who they were looking for.

* * *

Marion Mueller loved to entertain. Whether it was one of her famous formal charity dinners or her afternoon bridge game with the girls, she loved to add special touches to each event. Today was such a beautiful summer day she had decided to have her two table duplicate bridge game outside. The weather was perfect.

Actually, at eighty degrees, it was a little cool for July, but there was just a hint of a breeze and the fragrance of the lilacs in the front yard wafted across the front porch. The yellow two-story Cape Cod house, with a farmer's porch across the front, stood on the corner of Henry & Willow Streets. The house had been home to Marion Mueller for thirty five years. They bought it as an escape from the city and, when her husband passed away, she sold their Brownstone and moved in permanently. Michael had come home to live when he got his residency at Beth Israel Hospital. She was so proud she hung his certificate in her room, right next to his diplomas from Harvard and Rutgers.

Michael was staying at the hospital and had been for a few weeks. It was not unusual for him to be away for a prolonged period. He always claimed it was just his heavy work load, but Marion was sure he had a girl. She smiled as she carried a tray of iced tea, lemonade and brownies to the porch. She could not wait until the day he brought the young lady home.

"Okay girls, who had the tea and who had the lemonade?" She said placing the tray on an antique sideboard.

None of the ladies noticed the unmarked cars waiting at the end of both streets.

* * *

Paul Worton moved his right index finger slightly over the ribbed knob to adjust the high powered binoculars. He frowned as the silver haired woman came into focus. He moved his sight line up and down and around the entire house until he was back watching a group of eight elderly ladies laughing, playing cards and drinking iced tea.

"Shit!" he spat out. "This is going to suck one way or another."

"Yeah. No matter how we do this, those ladies are not going to know what hit them." The Suffolk County Police Captain said, as he lowered his field glasses.

"Look, Captain, this is your jurisdiction, but I wonder if we can take this slow and easy?" Worton said.

"We can do this however you want. I have known Tim Copeland for a long time and he filled us in a little on what is going on here. I have extra manpower and our tactical swat team available if you want to go that route. But for now, it is your show as to how you want to approach the house. I told Tim we would put the house under surveillance until you got here and we did. My men have seen no sign of any male presence at the house for the last eight hours. Really, no sign of life at all until about an hour ago when the ladies started to show up." The officer answered.

Worton stood by his unmarked car with Morales, Walsh, the Suffolk County Police captain and his SWAT team leader.

"Alright. Given the circumstances, it wasn't hard for Copeland to secure an arrest warrant for Mueller or a search warrant for his residence. I don't want to storm this house with those ladies sitting out front. But I also do not want to put them or any of your men at unnecessary risk." Worton said. He spoke again, this time to the SWAT team commander.

"Can you cover any escape route from the back or sides of the house?"

"Absolutely. We would need about twenty minutes to deploy." The man replied.

"Do it. And give us a heads up on the radio when you are in position, alright?" The SWAT team commander was on the move and spoke over his shoulder as he left.

"You got it." Worton turned to the police captain.

"Captain, can you cover us from the front? Move your men up both streets and place them where they can stay well hidden, but ready to go if needed?"

"Consider it done, but what are you going to do?" Worton looked at Morales and then Nicky Walsh.

"I guess we are going to join the tea party on the porch."

* * *

The King's Gambit

The Guggenheim Museum, located between 88th and 89th Streets on Fifth Avenue, is arguably the most unique building in New York City. Frank Lloyd Wright's inverted circular design of white stone stands out as a modernistic masterpiece on Manhattan's Upper East Side. Wright's vision did not become reality until October of 1959, nearly six months after his death. Though widely criticized by many purists at the time, The Guggenheim remains one of the world's greatest architectural marvels. Going against the age old, box-like structures that funnel visitors from room to room and from floor to floor in ascending manner, Wright's vision uses elevators to whisk its patrons to the top of the building, where they follow an ever-descending path to the foyer below. The one continuous wall along the way harbors the museum's art collection, along with small connecting exhibition rooms and sculpture laden alcoves. The initial criticism held that the building itself would take away from the famous art collection, but the ingenious design only adds to the artistic treasures it holds.

One of the highlights of any Guggenheim visit is standing in the middle of the main building's marble foyer and looking straight up. The walkway surrounds its visitors, extending upward in a ribbon of white to its widest point on the top floor forming overhead balconies along the way.

Michael Mueller rested his elbows on the railing to the top floor balcony and surveyed the activity below. From his vantage point, he could see the small decorative pool on one side of the foyer and the information booth straight across from it, the entrance to the museum and access to the gift shop centered along the wall to the left of the information booth. It was Michael's tenth, and final, trip to The Guggenheim before game six. Each time he arrived as a different tourist, never the same hair or complexion, never the same clothes, sometimes older, sometimes younger, sometimes with facial hair, sometimes without.

The changes at the museum were subtle. Only a trained eye would notice an extra person at the information desk or at the ticket counter. Any ordinary visitor would not know the difference between the regular employees and the undercover agents who quietly searched every inch of the great building. Only Michael Mueller knew the normal contingent of uniformed staff had doubled at The Guggenheim. He glanced casually as a young tour guide passed by. She smiled and talked, glowingly, about the museum. He knew her name was Nancy by the name tag above her left breast and he knew it was her birthday because of the paper crown she wore on her head.

Michael wondered who would wear a crown on the 27th. Would it be a worker or one of Paul Worton's team? Would he be able to get one of them alone? He used his cane to offset his exaggerated limp as he started the long walk along the descending ramp.

"Your move detective." He said.

* * *

Marion Mueller bid "two clubs" and waited for her partner's answering bid. She was sure they could make her bid and maybe even a slam if things fell right. As she took a sip of ice cold lemonade from her frosted glass she noticed three figures approaching the porch. It was a rare occurrence to see any strange face walking down Willow Street on a warm summer afternoon. Seeing three people, two of them in suit coats, just never happened. Her friends looked up from their card game as a puzzled Marion Mueller put her cards down and rose from her seat.

"We have visitors." She said.

Marion Mueller and Paul Worton reached the top of the porch steps at the same time. Detective Morales and Nicky Walsh stayed on each side of the lower steps. They paid no attention to the ladies on the porch. Their focus centered on the house and anyone who might be inside. The ladies were curious now. Some stood to get a better look, while the others just turned in their seats.

"Good afternoon Ma'am. I am Detective Paul Worton. I wonder if I could speak to you in private." Worton said. Marion

Mueller examined the credentials in Worton's left hand and then, tentatively, shook the right hand he had offered.

"What is this about officer?"

Worton glanced at the other ladies who were craning their necks with a little more interest than before.

"I really think it would be better to do this without an audience."

Suddenly, Marion Mueller's face went white. One hand covered her mouth while the other gripped the nearby banister to keep her from falling.

"Oh my God! It is Michael isn't it? What has happened to my son?" She sobbed.

"Nothing that I know of Ma'am, we are simply looking for Michael, if Michael Mueller is your son?" Worton said.

"Looking for him? What do you want with Michael?"

Worton shook his head and took a deep breath. Things were not going as he had hoped, but the time for small talk was over.

"Ma'am, I did not want to alarm you or these ladies. This house, in fact the entire neighborhood, is surrounded by police officers. I have a search warrant and I need to know right now whether Michael Mueller is in that house."

The older woman took a step back.

"No, Michael is not home. He has not been home for a more than a week. Sometimes he stays in the city for long periods, when the workload at the hospital is too much."

"What hospital, Ma'am? I was under the impression that your son worked at The Mohegan Sun Resort."

Marion Mueller gave a hint of a condescending smile.

"Oh no, Officer Michael works at Beth Israel Hospital in the city. He is a surgeon." She explained.

* * *

Two hours later, Paul Worton left a bewildered Marion Mueller sitting on her front porch. For Worton, it had been a painful two hours. He had seen Marion Mueller's world crumble with each word he spoke.

Her son was not a heart surgeon at Beth Israel Hospital. In fact, he was not a doctor at all. He had never completed his residency and did not have a license to practice medicine. She had no knowledge of her son's activities as a stage performer, a ski instructor, a bounty hunter, or a personnel trainer. She was incredulous when informed that her son had worked for two years as a blackjack dealer, while she believed him to be saving lives in an operating room. But the worst came when Worton told her why they were looking for her son. He had to tell her in order to serve the warrant to search the house.

She sat in a trance and answered every question, while allowing them to search the house after her friends helped her read the warrant. She told of her husband's obsession with chess and his hopes for his son's future. She told of his disappointment with her son's failure and of his death from prostate cancer. And every few minutes, she told him he must be mistaken. Michael could never hurt anyone.

Worton took a deep breath as he walked to the car. He had spent the afternoon ruining an older woman's quiet life and he did not feel he was any closer to his killer.

* * *

GAME 6

July 27th

"You may analyze ten or twenty moves ahead, the possibilities branch out. Every six moves has at least six possibilities for each move."
Shelby Lyman

Andy Wiley was not nearly as confident of his future as he was ten days earlier. Things had changed dramatically from the moment he fell into the Carnegie Hall murder story. At first, the story jolted his name and face to the head of the class for up and coming young journalists, but he did not have time to bask in the limelight before the killer contacted him. His instant excitement quickly mixed with fear. If the killer could hack into his computer with ease, what else could he do?

The fear disappeared in waves of new found popularity.

To tell what he knew on the air, he had to tell his boss how he got the information. That meeting led to a bigger meeting. Every big wig connected with Channel 4, along with the station's lawyers, met to determine what the next step would be. They, of course, would use the story. The great composer's sudden death was the biggest news story of the year and Channel 4 had access to information that no one else had. The lawyers assured them that what they were doing was legal and that neither Andy or the station were under any obligation to divulge the source of their information.

That night Andy Wiley went on air for the first time armed with clues and pictures supplied directly by a murderer. The following morning he was in a police station interview room, accompanied by lawyers who answered every question by claiming Andy had a right to protect his source. Though they threatened him with jail time, he was finally released and headed home.

That night, a call came from the Chief Editor of *The Daily News*. How soon could he throw together a column for the paper concerning "The Chessboard Killer", and would he be interested in his own private office and a weekly byline?

The next day, he was back on the air to tell the world that New York City had a serial killer on its hands. He described the death in Union Square and the hanging of a professor at The American Academy for Dramatic Arts.

The killer had contacted him again.

Now he sat in the dark of his small apartment looking out on the lights of New York City. He was torn between his desire for the story and what many would consider his moral duty.

The Police Commissioner for the City of New York called his good friend and political ally, Rodney McKnight. McKnight owned a fifty-one percent share in the Channel 4 News Station. The Commissioner asked for a meeting between his investigative task force, the station manager, the station lawyers and Andy Wiley.

McKnight agreed.

The meeting took place uptown at the 18th Precinct, in a large conference room. Wiley, his boss and his lawyers were introduced to the Precinct Squad Commander, Tim Copeland and Detective Paul Worton. Copeland made it clear that the city had a court order that could land Wiley in jail for obstruction of justice. But he quickly followed that threat with an offer of information for information.

Wiley and his boss met privately with Lieutenant Copeland and Detective Worton. For the next hour, the two police investigators brought the two men up to date on their investigation of four murders and one attempted murder over the last ten days. They told of bizarre clues at each scene and the killer's obsession with the game of chess. He glanced quickly at Detective Worton when Lieutenant Copeland mentioned that the killer had contacted the police detective directly. He recognized the edge in his voice when Worton told them that one of his men was the fourth victim. Finally, they told him they believed the killer had contacted him and given him the information he was reporting. Lieutenant Copeland asked for his help. Copeland told him they would rather work with him than put him in jail and asked him to go home and think it over.

Now his fear was back.

Andy Wiley knew he could still report the story if he helped. He knew he would be famous and he knew no other news outlet would be able to scoop this story. But he was wary now. In fact, he was scared.

He glanced across the darkened room at the red "**click me**" light blinking in the bottom left hand corner of his computer screen.

If he helped the cops, would he become a victim?

* * *

Paul Worton looked at his watch. *3:15PM, July 26th.* They were as prepared as could be but would it be enough to catch Mueller?

Under massive protests from the trustees, The Guggenheim Museum was closed to the public from midnight July 26th until 9:00 a.m. the following morning. If Worton had his way, the museum would be closed to the public on the 27th as well. He tried to convince his boss that they could prevent another killing by simply keeping everyone out of the building until 12:01 on the 28th.

But Tim Copeland wanted a capture and felt The Guggenheim was their best chance so far. No reason was given for the museum closure and no person would be allowed inside until employees arrived for work the next day. The screening process awaiting every person entering the building would be nothing short of airport security lines. Undercover cops would work alongside regular staff members.

Three Guggenheim workers were surprised and happy when told they would not have to wear the normally mandatory paper crowns designated for employees on their birthday. Task Force detectives would wear the paper crowns in their place, along with staff uniforms. At a final briefing, everyone involved received a recent picture and complete dossier on suspect Michael Mueller.

Worton picked up the photo and stared at the smiling image in his hand. Mueller was handsome, almost pretty, in a tough kind of way. He was tan, tall and athletic.

Worton leaned back in the oversized easy chair. The leather chair, end table and floor lamp created a reading area in the far right hand corner of the den. The den itself featured wall to ceiling dark mahogany wood panels. The antique designed hardwood floors featured a braided rug with a matching mahogany desk, centered in front of a large bay window. The den was Worton's sanctuary. The place he went when he needed to think and concentrate. He opened the file on Michael Mueller and started reading for the third time.

After leaving Victor Menchenko's tutoring and entering Sag Harbor Elementary School, Michael seemed to lead a fairly normal life. Actually, the report lifted a few eyebrows because of how boring it was. It showed no involvement in any school activity including the high school chess club. The only significant event was the death of his father when the boy was fifteen. He graduated first in his class but was not valedictorian. Nor did he garner any specific awards or scholarships. Administrators at the school reported that Mueller certainly would have been eligible for scholastic scholarship, but that he never applied.

The King's Gambit

His early acceptance at Harvard was a first for the school, but he did not even attend his graduation. The statements from Harvard and Rutgers were much the same. Excellent grades but no social activities. No girlfriends to speak of, in fact no real friends at all. Those who remembered him recalled a friendly, quiet, intelligent boy who fit in fine with everyone, but never stood out. No one interviewed remembered ever seeing him play chess or remembered him talking about chess.

Finally, one teacher at Rutgers remembered that Michael could most often be found in the library during his spare time. What investigators found was a very short list of books on Mueller's library card. He always took one of five books out over a two year period while attending Rutgers Medical School. He always spent four or five hours in the library and returned the book of choice before he left. The list included *Bobby Fischer Teaches Chess, My 60 Memorable Games*, both written by Fischer. *Fischer-his Approach to Chess*, written by Elie Augur, *Match of the Century*, written by Robert White and *Chess: A Celebration of 2,000 Years*, written by Roswin Finkenzeller, Wilheim Ziehr and Emil M. Buhrer.

Law enforcement received statements about Mueller, from the time he left school until he returned home to Sag Harbor, and they all sounded exactly the same. No criminal record, no long term relationships, no trouble of any kind. He was a hard worker and avid learner. He became a makeup artist while working in Summer Stock Theater. A club squash champion and the number one personal trainer at his health club in Colorado. A police station junkie and expert marksman, while on the job as a bounty hunter in California. He then returned home to take a job dealing blackjack at The Mohegan Sun Casino. All the while, leading his mother to believe he was a surgeon at Beth Israel Hospital in the city.

The bank records showed a trust fund balance of close to thirty million dollars when Michael took charge of it two years earlier. His first order of business was to transfer one million to a checking account and to withdraw five hundred thousand dollars in cash. All interest from the Trust Fund would be transferred monthly to his mother's checking account. Each month, for the last two years, Michael Mueller withdrew two hundred thousand dollars in cash from the trust fund. The total amount withdrawn equaled almost five million dollars, none of which had ever been deposited in the checking account. So far, no record could be found of what happened to the money. No bank account in Mueller's name had been located anywhere in the United States or abroad.

Outside of the people at the casino, the people at the bank and his mother's immediate friends, no one seemed to know Michael Mueller.

On July 10th, Michael filled out papers taking his name off the trust fund and the checking account, leaving control of the remaining twenty-five million dollars in his mother's name.

No one had seen him since.

Worton closed the folder and picked up the picture one more time.

"I know where you will be tomorrow, but who will you be?" He said to the image he held.

The door to the den opened with a knock and his fourteen year old daughter stuck her head around the edge of the door.

"Dad, you got a minute?" She asked.

"Sure kiddo. What's up?" He said stuffing the picture in the folder.

Jacqueline Worton nearly ran across the room to lean over the arm of her dad's chair, talking as fast as she moved.

"Well a bunch of the kids from the team are going to the beach this Saturday and having a clambake and stuff. I don't have any games or practice and I really want to go. We're gonna swim and play volleyball and just have a ball. So, can I go, huh?"

"Whoa kiddo! Wait a minute. Who's going? What time? What beach? What did your mom say?"

Jackie's smile faded quickly. She shifted her feet and screwed up her face.

"I haven't asked her. I told her I would help her at the store this weekend, but I didn't know about the party back then. I thought maybe you could talk to her."

Worton stood and hugged his daughter.

"You know it doesn't work like that around here, Kiddo. If you committed to her, you have to honor that commitment. If you have a good reason and she can get by without you, she probably will let you go." He paused and lifted her chin so she could see his eyes. "That's if we like the answers to my other questions."

"Questions to what?" Lori Worton asked, as she walked in the room. "You guys got a conspiracy going here?"

"No conspiracy here. Jackie was just looking for you. Right kiddo?"

"Yeah, okay Dad."

"Well, don't look so glum, Honey. It can't be that bad." Lori said.

Paul Worton picked up the file and grabbed his suit coat.

"I'll leave you guys to it. I have to run. Not sure when I will be home again. I will give you a call."

He kissed his daughter on the forehead and gave Lori a hug. She hugged him back and kissed him.

"The Guggenheim?" She asked.

"Yeah."

"Be careful."

When he left the den, his daughter was pleading her case to his wife. What he wouldn't give to stay home with them and deal with a beach party problem.

* * *

Victor Menchenko's apartment was way above upscale, even for New York City. Between tuition collected for private tutoring, book deals, appearance fees and endorsements, Victor had become a very rich man. He was used to the very best of everything and he had the game of chess to thank for every bit of his good fortune, but not today.

Victor Menchenko picked up the white ivory chess piece. He loved the feel of the heavy, smooth game piece in his hand. He rolled it between his fingers and wondered if this nightmare scenario could really be true.

The second he heard the name Michael Mueller, he remembered the boy and his father. Many a family brought their son or daughter to Victor Menchenko's monthly workshops, hoping their child would become the next protégé to the Great Grandmaster. Those students that passed through to his private tutoring got full value for the steep price they paid. The accomplishments of Victor's students ranged from local monthly tournament victories, to Grandmasters competing in The World Championship. Over the years, his students competed and won in elementary, high school and national amateur events, culminating in six U.S. Champions and four U.S. Open winners. Two of his students actually achieved Grandmaster status and competed in International events. But the anguish associated with young Michael Mueller and his obsessive father was hard to forget.

Victor Menchenko told the police of Jefferson Mueller's obsession with Bobby Fischer and his desire to have his son meet, if not surpass, the records of America's great champion. He told of countless frustrated teaching sessions and tournament failures. He told of the father's anguish and the boy's pleas for one more chance, when he informed Jefferson Mueller that the boy was just not good enough. They both left his office in tears. He never saw them again.

Now he had a police officer stationed outside his apartment door and two more on the street below.

He was well aware that his apartment at Tacy Towers, on 24th Street and Second Avenue, sat right in the middle of the ten block area designated for the tenth, and final, victim in Michael Mueller's bizarre chess game.

The King's Gambit

* * *

Alexandra Jenkins was on the job and she was excited like she had not been in years. She left home to make it on Broadway at the age of seventeen and three years later was one of the highest paid escort ladies in New York City. Alex, as her friends and clients called her, long ago learned to block out her everyday life from her job. The agency's client research and employee protection was exemplary. Her pay earned her a six figure salary and she lived a lifestyle she had never dreamed of. The drawback, of course, was once the agency gave her a client and she accepted, she was committed to the client and his wishes.

Some nights she simply had to represent herself as someone she was not, at a concert or art show. Other nights she had to fake her way through a high class party and put up with some drunken groping. The worst nights were the same as they were three years ago. Clients bought her services for the night and that included her body, if so desired. She was paid to deliver what they asked for and it was rarely simple straight- forward sex. But today was different.

The client was very specific and, at first glance, Alex was sure she would be in for a long, kinky night. He contacted the agency two weeks earlier and requested a pretty petite woman who would be available on July the 27th for a full twenty four hours, starting at 9 a.m. The kicker was, he wanted someone who actually was born on July 27th and Alex fit the bill. As she stood in front of Artie's Deli on the corner of 82nd and 3rd Avenue, she had visions of herself dressed in child's clothes, at a warped, sex crazed, birthday party.

At exactly nine o'clock, a man approached her. He was a bit older, but good looking and polite. He offered her a cup of coffee and explained why he had hired her for the day. He told her she had the perfect look and asked to see proof that it was, indeed, her birthday. In three years, it was the most surprising and so far the most enjoyable day she had spent with a client. She would get to do a little acting and he would pay her an extra thousand dollars the agency would never know about.

It was mid-morning when paid escort Alexandra Jenkins, dressed as a young tourist, approached the front entrance of The Guggenheim Museum with Michael Mueller.

* * *

Paul Worton stood by a small semi-circular pool in the white marble lobby of The Guggenheim Museum. The crowd had been steady from the time the doors opened and people started working their way through the intense security checks. Only two tourists came close to matching the description or picture of Michael Mueller, but nothing had come of it. Check points throughout the building called in at fifteen minute intervals, but nothing out of the ordinary had been reported.

Worton knew the drill. According to Nuge and the rest of his task force, there were four more dates in Michael Muller's bizarre chess game, after The Guggenheim. Seven days from now, on August 3rd, then again on August 6th, 10th and, finally, August 31st, the killer would act again. It seemed evident that Victor Menchenko would be the final target. He lived in the right target area and his dismissal of the young chess player seemed to have been the trigger point for Michael Mueller's vendetta. He was under round-the-clock police protection. The other three locations were much more problematic. One was basically in the middle of Times Square. Another seemed to indicate a murder in or around Penn Station and a third showed no particular standout landmark. The Task Force would work day and night to narrow down a target for each date, but the task was not getting any easier. Copeland was right. They needed Mueller to show himself here at The Guggenheim. Worton checked his watch, 11:00 a.m. Thirteen hours to go. His phone rang.

"Worton here."

"Good morning, Detective. It has been a few days since we last spoke and you have been quite busy." Michael Mueller said.

"What do you want Michael?"

The silence on the other end of the phone told Worton that Mueller was not prepared for his identity to be known. He decided to push his advantage.

"Your mother defended you for as long as she could. Even in the face of overwhelming evidence, she still wanted to believe you were a practicing physician instead of a murderer."

"She will survive this. She will play cards and plan another benefit within weeks. She will never want for anything." Mueller said. His voice was quiet as if trying to convince himself.

"The last time I saw her, she was in shock. I felt sorry for her. Her dream for her son seemed crushed." Worton persisted.

"Enough, Detective what is done is done. You are further along than I anticipated. I will have to take that under advisement. But, I did not call to discuss my mother. I called to commend you on your play in today's game. I had not anticipated that you would close the museum all day yesterday. I assume all entrances are manned and the building is as secure as possible. Well played, Detective, though hardly fair. How can I play if I cannot get in?" Mueller asked. His voice was back to normal. He was enjoying himself again.

"Fair! Are you serious? You killed four people before we even knew we were involved in the so-called game and it was pure luck that we stopped the fifth one." Worton said with disgust.

"Luck? Yes, dropping the remote was a serious blunder." Mueller paused for a second. "Of course! You got a fingerprint from the remote how foolish of me."

"Listen Mueller. You have lost. We know who you are and we will catch you at some point. Maybe if we had never found your identity you could have gotten away with this. Yeah, I admit the idea is brilliant, using the city as a chess board, but you can't walk away from this now. Why not let the last five victims live? What you have done will be remembered for a long time no matter what and, let's face it, that was your goal: to prove something to your Dad and to be remembered for it."

"Nice try, Detective, but the match is still on. I will see you in seven days. We will find out if you are very lucky, or very skilled." Mueller said.

The line went dead.

"Shit!" Worton swore at the phone in his hand. Quickly, he switched to his hand held receiver.

"All units, be on alert. He is here or he is going to try to get in. I would bet my life on it."

* * *

Michael Mueller snapped his cell phone shut. From the shadows on the top tier of balconies high above The Guggenheim rotunda, he watched Detective Paul Worton. He was wary now. Worton was a tougher opponent than he could have hoped, which only made the match more intriguing. But he must be careful. It was an obvious risk to come to The Guggenheim under the current conditions. But his plan had worked. His female escort played the role of his granddaughter expertly and the disguises worked perfectly, letting them slip through the security check quickly. Now he had decisions to make.

First and foremost, could he execute his game plan and escape from the Museum without losing the match? Would it be better to concede this game and move on to game six? No. The game was still there for the taking and it was his move and it was time to get the pieces moving. He stepped into a small, lighted alcove where Alex Jenkins stood admiring a sixteenth century Greek sculpture.

"Ready to have some fun and make a couple of bucks?" He asked with a grin.

The King's Gambit

"Let's do it." She said, as she turned to him with her most engaging smile. If he only knew, she thought. For a thousand dollars she would have worn the paper crown naked.

* * *

Detective Morales spotted the birthday crown before he noticed the young woman wearing it. She was making her way down the last spiral ramp leading to the rotunda floor. The woman was not one of the three undercover cops designated to wear the decoy crowns.

Morales had been monitoring call-ins from every check point in the building when the paper crown caught his eye. He shut the receiver down and let out a short sharp whistle to get Worton's attention. The woman stopped in the middle of the rotunda floor. Alex Jenkins folded her arms and waited.

Worton spoke into a small hand mike as he and Morales moved towards the woman.

"All parties, be on the alert. We have an unidentified woman in the foyer wearing one of these birthday crowns. She is not one of us, or a Guggenheim employee. This is Mueller's work. Look for anything suspicious."

Morales stood to one side, keeping Worton and the woman in his sites. His hand slipped inside his jacket to the Glock 9mm on his belt, as Worton reached the woman. Alex smiled and reached out her hand.

"You must be Paul. Michael says Happy Birthday."

"It is not my birthday lady. Where is Mueller?" Worton said. Alex's smile disappeared.

"I don't understand. Michael said it was your birthday too."

"I am a Homicide Detective, Miss, and you need to tell me exactly what Michael Mueller told you to do and you need to tell me now. He is here to kill someone, maybe you. Now start talking." Paul Worton said. The fear in Alex Jenkin's eyes was as real as the sick feeling in her stomach. She had dealt with cops before and knew this guy meant business.

"I work for an escort service and this guy called and wanted someone to make his brother's fiftieth birthday memorable. Give him a girl for the night that was born on the same day. We were going to sneak in so his brother didn't recognize him and then I was to come down here wearing the crown and surprise him. That's all I know. He said his brother's name was Paul. I was supposed to meet him here."

"Where did you last see him?"

Jennifer slowly lifted her eyes upward past each circular tier to the top of the building. Worton's eyes followed.

"Up there." She said

* * *

Allen Ricker was one of those rare employees who genuinely loved his job. As a graduate student at the New York Academy of Art and a tour guide at The Guggenheim, his life's passion melded with a source of much needed income. It allowed him the sheer joy of introducing some of the world's most renowned collections to the general public.

As usual, Allen took his lunch break in one of the many alcoves sprinkled along each of the ribboned tiers of the museum. Bottled water and a granola bar would suffice while he inspected, or took notes on the latest object of his curiosity. He could sit and stare at the intricacies of fine sculptures, or the lines and hues of great paintings, for hours. Today he had ventured to the fifth floor to view The Guggenheim's newest acquisition, a collection titled "Arcadia & Anarchy, Divisionism/Neo-Impressionism". The paintings of the Italian Divisionism artists from the turn of the 19th century would only be on display until August 6th. Time was short and Allen was not ready to leave when the alarm on his wristwatch signaled the end of his hour break. Duty called, so he buttoned his shirt, fixed his tie and reached for his uniform jacket. He looked up, startled to find a figure looming over him.

* * *

Six months earlier, when Michael Mueller started his canvas of The Guggenheim Museum, he targeted Allen Ricker. It was an easy choice. Ricker was the only male employee at the museum whose birthday fell on July 27th. It was his day to wear the crown. Michael once again had to give kudos to Detective Worton. The defensive positions undertaken to get the upper hand in game six were strong: closing the museum for the entire day on the 26th to prepare, under-cover police officers wearing the birthday crowns, intense screening of every person entering the front doors and officers posted throughout the building. All good strategic moves, but not good enough to thwart Michael's counter moves. And Worton had made a serious blunder. A mistake as bad as Michael's own miscue, when he dropped the remote in game five.

He let the three birthday employees come to work today. If he kept them home, game six would be over. Worton should have known that Michael would know everything about his victim before seeing him wearing the paper crown. Thinking Ricker was safe because he did not actually wear the crown, meant nothing. It was Ricker's birthday and he was "King" for the day. He was about to be checkmated.

The girl would be in the lobby by now and things would start moving very fast. Michael covered the distance from his spot in front of a painting to the alcove in three quick strides.

A woman's voice inside the alcove stopped him in his tracks. She was obviously talking to someone on a phone or remote receiver because he could only hear one voice.

"Yes sir. I have him secured and he is not resisting. Both units are nearby and closing fast. No sir, they report little activity up here. Just a group of teenagers with a chaperone and an old man… I don't know. I have not seen him, but they said he was about five-eight, stooped shoulders and using a cane to walk." She said, in spaced intervals.

Michael heard all he needed to hear. He scrunched down, put his cane to the floor and shuffled off in the direction he had come. At the first corner, he slipped into the men's room. His mind was racing as he ripped the wig from his head and the beard from his face. Moments later, he climbed on the sink and used his cane to prop open the slanted window high above the tile floor. He then jumped and caught the sill by his fingertips and, using all his strength, pulled his body up and out, onto a stone walkway just outside the window. He grabbed his cane, closed the window and, for a moment, sat hunched over trying to catch his breath.

Worton had used Allen Ricker as a decoy. He knew all along that Michael would target the tour guide. This time it was no blunder that foiled his plan. This time Worton was one move ahead and that worried him. Mueller pushed Worton and his own failure from his mind. He had to escape. He had to put his fall-back plan in motion. Quickly, he started his decent from the museum's exterior facade.

Inside the building, Worton stood in the middle of the marble foyer. He pressed the button on his remote.

"All units, be on the look-out for an old man who looks to be seventy to eighty years old with white hair and grey beard. He is stooped at the waist, using a cane, approach with caution. Check every inch of this place. Every broom closet and bathroom. Do not let him out of this building. If I am right, the old man is Mueller and he is desperate to get out."

* * *

GAME 7

August 3rd

"Each game, as it takes place, has constant confrontations. You can look at a chess board and see pieces attacking and defending opponents that are always counter-attacking."

Shelby Lyman

"God damn! We had him twice now. First, he hides in a janitor's closet right next to us and we don't break the door down and check it out. Then, yesterday, he is in the building. We set a trap for him. He falls for it and he still gets away. How Paul? How? Tell me again."

Every other member of the Task Force sat quietly, thanking God that they were not the center of Lieutenant Commander Tim Copeland's attention. But Paul Worton knew his boss. He knew, even though the Squad Commander was steaming, it was frustration talking rather than anger. Copeland was a take charge guy. A get things done guy and the "Chess Board Killer", as the media had dubbed him, had Copeland as frustrated as Worton had ever seen him.

"Boss, no one is to blame about the screw up in the park except me. I was in the room. I tried the door. It was locked. It never dawned on me that he might be in there and it should have." Worton said.

"Yesterday we did everything we could to catch him and he out-smarted us. In case of trouble he had a preplanned escape route ready and executed it perfectly. We found his wig, fake beard, and the clothes he had on when he entered the museum behind a trash bin in a fifth floor men's room. Scuff marks on a sink and the window sill above it show where he got out. There is a flat part on the roof right below the window. He must have stashed a rope and harness on the roof when he cased the place. Our guys found the climber's rope hanging off the back of the building about an hour after we caught Alexandra Jenkins, his call-girl decoy. We had the doors and fire escapes covered but, quite frankly, we weren't looking outside or up at that point. By the time we did, he was gone." Worton paused for a moment. "Again it sucks, but for the second time we prevented him from killing his target and that is our number one job."

Tim Copeland paced the length of the room as Worton spoke. Now he stopped in front of the assembled Task Force. His voice was calm and level when he spoke.

"Okay. Where do we go next?"

Worton glanced at Ray Pearson. The Behavioral Science expert opened a folder and began to speak.

"Mueller has four dates left on his game list, for want of a better phrase. August 3rd, 6th, and then September 1st. We know, well we don't know, but everything points to Victor Menchenko being his final target. This whole chess fixation and need to prove his worth, seems to stem from his failure under Menchenko's tutelage. Menchenko is the one who told him he was not good enough and Menchenko lives in the grid for the September 1st attack."

Tim Copeland broke in.

"We have Menchenko covered twenty four-seven from now until after midnight on the 1st. What else?"

"Yes, but he has three other victims targeted right now. We know from the first six attacks that he does extensive research and has tremendous resources. Finding out who and exactly where he will attack, is nearly impossible unless we get lucky. We are combing every possible site, interviewing every possible target and will be ready at the most predominate sites in each grid. That has been his M.O. with the exception of the park in Spanish Harlem and we just don't think he could find a better place up there. The problem with the next three grids is that we are dealing with places like Rockefeller Center, Central Park and Penn Station." The profiler said.

Pearson's words hung in the air. Finally, Tim Copeland spoke.

"Let's get after it then. The best we can do is leave nothing to chance. But, if he gets as far as September 1st, we cannot be complacent with Menchenko, even if we are in the room with him. This guy will try to get to him no matter what. He is that arrogant, that confident." Copeland warned.

"I will be in the room with Menchenko if it comes to that." Paul Worton said.

The two men stared at each other for a moment. Then Copeland walked briskly to the conference room door and opened it.

"Let's get him before that shall we?" he said, as the door closed behind him.

* * *

Michael Mueller hunkered down in the secluded room behind his bedroom wall to contemplate the events of the last two games. He had barely escaped capture twice. For a moment, he thought he might not have what it takes. He did not look at Fischer's picture on the wall. Maybe the professor was right all those years ago. He could hear those crushing words again.

"Michael is not good enough. He never will be."

"Not good enough."

"Not good enough."

Suddenly, he stood and screamed at the giant poster of Bobby Fischer on the wall.

"Stop wallowing in self pity!"

He was no young boy. He was Michael Mueller. He was second to none, including Menchenko and even Fischer. He had set plans in motion with extensive strategies. Made moves way ahead of his opponent which allowed him to escape both games with a stalemate instead of a capture. No, he was still in command. He would credit a fine opponent and then bury him in game seven.

Michael Mueller turned on his Blackberry and started to type a message. It was time to jack up the pressure.

* * *

Andy Wiley took a deep breath. He was moments away from fame like he had never known and possibly a trip to jail. Karen Meadows, on the anchor desk, was just about finished with her lead-in to his introduction.

His last communiqué from Michael Mueller was eye popping. The information was extensive and exclusive. He made his decision. He could not pass up the chance to blow open the biggest crime story of the year, maybe of the last ten years. His column would hit the streets before the morning commute and he would be on the air in minutes. Andy was no longer worried that he might be in danger. He reasoned that if Mueller killed him he would have to find a new source to help make him famous.

Andy sat quietly in the tall swivel chair, letting the station make-up artist put the finishing touches on his face. She stepped away at the last moment, as the green light appeared on the camera in front of Andy.

"Good evening. My Name is Andy Wiley. This is an exclusive report on the so-called "Chess Board Murders." So far, four people are dead and two more have narrowly escaped the clutches of this diabolical killer. Starting on July 11th, with the brutal murder of maestro Vincent Antonelli at Carnegie Hall, the New

York City Police Department has been engaged in a deadly game of cat and mouse with the most complex serial killer since "The Son of Sam."

"Mr. Antonelli was stabbed to death with his own baton on July 11th. Two days later, on July 13th, the president of the Long Island Railroad's division of the Teamsters Union, Jorge Gonzalez, was poisoned in broad daylight while eating breakfast in Union Square. On July 16th, renowned Professor Clifford Davenport was found hanged in the foyer of The American Academy of Performing Arts and on July 20th, young Police Detective Anthony Austin was cut down just inside the entrance to the New York City Police Academy Training Center. Since that time, the police have thwarted attacks on gang lord Angel Vargas in Spanish Harlem and on a tour guide at The Guggenheim Museum."

Andy paused for effect.

"These are not random killings. They are coordinated moves in a bizarre chess game that the killer, identified as one Michael Mueller, has instigated against New York's finest. Mueller has divided the nine cross streets and avenues of this great city into a giant chess board. He has left a clue at each crime scene. A paper diagram of a chess board showing that game's crime scene."

"The authorities have used these clues to determine the dates and the ten block area for each attack. They know he has four more dates on his schedule and four more intended victims."

"They have stopped him twice. But can they stop him four more times and will they ever catch the most famous American chess player since Bobby Fischer?"

"We, here at Channel 4, feel it is our duty to warn the public about these vicious attacks and to make you aware that four more attacks are imminent. As more information becomes available we will continue to bring it to your attention. You can get a more detailed account of "The Chess Board Murders Case" in my column in tomorrow's morning edition of *The Daily News*."

"This is Andy Wiley, with a Channel 4 special report."

Paul Worton watched Andy Wiley's image on the flat screen TV set up in the corner of his den. He inhaled a long, deep breath and held it. Slowly, he blew the air out through his teeth, closing his eyes and leaning back until the black leather easy chair reached full extension. He sat with one leg draped over the arm of the chair and both arms hanging by his sides. Lori stood, arms folded in the doorway.

"We are in deep shit now. The big boys have been badgering Copeland about this case. So far he has kept them off my back. But after that report they are going to want my head on a platter."

Lori left the doorway and walked to her husband's side. She took the remote and hit the "off" button. She leaned over, kissed his lips and took him by the hand.

"Come to bed with me while some of the good parts are still left." She said.

* * *

Night or day, winter or summer, Rockefeller Center may be the most popular tourist attraction in New York City. The streets and walkways around the sunken rectangular skating ring are thick with sightseers. In the summer months, passers-by look down on umbrella tops stretching tip to tip across the once frozen expanse. One story down, under the fluttering wave of flags from every nation, patrons partake of food and drink from the menus and bars of Rockefeller Center's four star restaurants.

Michael Mueller walked casually past the glass elevator at the entrance to Rockefeller Center. He could look down Fifth Avenue, past the statue of Atlas guarding the front door of the International Building, to the looming spires of St. Patrick's Cathedral. He glanced left across the sunken plaza, now serving as an outdoor restaurant, past the golden statue of Prometheus, to the RCA Building. Turning left into the plaza, he could see Studio One's "Window on the World" on the far opposite corner of 49th Street. Every morning this section of the city was packed with fans straining against ropes to see the stars and guests of NBC's Today Show. To his right, he glanced up at the towering facade of 30 Rockefeller Center. The mammoth skyscraper serves as home to many of the world's largest companies including Time Warner, General Electric, the Associated Press and the NBC Studios. Many patrons visit Rockefeller Center for a trip to the renowned Rainbow Bar and Grill at the top of the great building. To his left, the perimeter of the dormant rink is crowded, except for the railing directly opposite the massive stone entrance. For an extra added attraction on summer nights, Rockefeller Center becomes an outdoor movie theater with an oversized picture screen rising high above the edge of the dormant rink.

Michael made his way to one of several round, wooden benches located between the entrance to the G. E. Building and the screen. He leaned back against the wooden slats and let his head touch the tips of the white and yellow daisies flowing from the middle of the circular planters. Michael drank in the sweet aroma of the long stemmed flowers. He knew he was taking a chance coming here just a day before game seven but he wanted one last look at the game board. He was satisfied. His shaved head, small goatee, tank top, shorts, and sandals assured his anonymity, and he was pretty sure that Paul Worton would not guess this location. Michael smiled. Even if Worton somehow stumbled on the site, he would never guess tomorrow night's "King". Mueller looked straight across the dormant rink, past the golden statue, and up the street between the buildings directly in front of him. He was more than satisfied.

Michael stood and walked to the end of the plaza, planning to retrace his steps north up 5th Avenue. He froze, as Detective Paul Worton stepped out of the passenger door of a black sedan parked in front of the elevators. He turned slowly towards St. Patrick's, lifting the camera from around his neck in a pretense of taking a picture. Worton actually brushed his back as he passed onto Rockefeller Plaza. Michael continued to snap photos, turning as he did toward the detective and his entourage. There were three men and one woman with him. Michael sucked in his breath when they came to a stop at the wooden bench he was sitting on moments before.

Worton did most of the talking and Michael relaxed. They were probably checking a hundred different places and they never even looked at the bench. Yet he had not expected Worton to be in the bathroom by the park, or to use the tour guide as a decoy at The Guggenheim. He must not underestimate this player again. Michael continued to watch the group as he moved to stand with the crowd milling about the railing overlooking the ice rink. He knew he should leave the area immediately, but he just could not resist. He smiled again as he reached into his pocket.

* * *

Paul Worton answered his phone on the second ring.

"Good afternoon, Detective." Mueller said.

"Mueller. I wondered when you would call." Worton said. "Then again, after a couple of failures, you might not have had much to say."

"Failures? Yes, in your eyes I can understand your choice of words. But in a chess match, a loss, though never welcome, is a matter of fact in championship competition. A great player must be able to accept a loss or a stalemate and move on to the next game. If he is really championship caliber, he will learn something from each contest that he can use against his opponent when next they meet."

Mueller never took his eyes off Paul Worton as he spoke. He felt a tremendous adrenaline rush. Here he was standing fifty yards away from the man assigned to catch him and he could not feel safer. He was one of more than two hundred people in, or around, Rockefeller Center and thirty had to be on cell phones.

"Please stop referring to this as a game. It obviously serves your purpose to do so and I will try to think in terms of chess to stop you if it helps. But this is no game, Mueller. You are a murderer, no different than any other serial killer who has convinced himself that his crusade justifies his actions."

"Why do you resort to insults Detective? It will not help you to win. Game seven is tomorrow and I am sure you are hard at work trying to locate the site. Every game against the same opponent is harder than the last. Even if you were to find where I will attack next, it would take someone with Grandmaster skills to save game seven's King."

There was silence on the other end for a second. Mueller watched as Worton dropped his hand to his side leaving the phone dangling from his hand. The detective did a slow turn watching the crowd as he did. A pang of fear shot through Mueller. Something had changed. Worton was looking for him. Something he said tipped the detective off. He kept the phone to his ear, but slipped into the crowd moving east on 51st Street.

"Spread out. I think Mueller is here watching us while he talks to me." Worton said to his team, before raising the phone back to his ear.

Mueller was deep in thought trying to determine what the detective had picked up on when Worton's voice startled him.

"It is not an insult if it is true. You are no different than any other common murderer or terrorist. You kill innocent people to justify an ends to a means. At least terrorists have some warped belief that they are doing some good. You are just playing games. But your buddy, Fischer, would probably approve. From what I understand, he turned into a nut case just like you. You know he hates this country now. He said 9/11 was a good thing and Hitler was a great man. He even denounces all Jews, even though his mother was Jewish. Nice! It must be wonderful to have a guy like him as a hero?"

"I never said he was my hero. I never said I agreed with his political views. But he was the greatest American chess player of all time until now!" Mueller, spat into the phone.

"Are you serious? Kasparov would have slapped Fischer around the table if Fischer didn't run and hide in Japan for twenty years."

Mueller was fuming. He wanted to stop and scream into the phone. But he slowed his breathing and continued to move with the crowd. Worton was trying to goad him into making a mistake. When he spoke his voice was calm.

"Every chess player knows that Kasparov was a poor man's Fischer and I am much too good a player to allow my game to be affected by insults. Your attempt to throw me off is noted Detective. You are a worthy opponent and I understand your frustration. It is good to see a man who is proud of the place he lives and wants to protect it and I am sure the place you live is proud of you, but I am focused on tomorrow. I certainly hope you are, because you will need to be perfect to win game seven."

The line went dead and Paul Worton stood alone on the stone plaza of Rockefeller Center.

* * *

Henry Windsor pushed his cart to the middle of the bronze colored marble floor just inside the entrance to 30 Rockefeller Center. He rested his chin on top of his hands and leaned on the mop handle. Henry worked the midnight to eight shift on the first ten floors of the building and this was his favorite spot. He was not sure if the characterizations painted on the gleaming walls and ceilings depicted mythological or medieval figures. He did not know if they represented famous people in history, or certain moments in time. He only knew that the colors and drawings fascinated him. Every night he stopped in this spot to let his imagination take him to places he would never go.

The King's Gambit

The hand held radio crackled in the holster on his belt.

"Hey King, are you gonna play poker at break today?" a voice asked.

Henry Windsor had been called "King Henry" since his high school days. Henry starred in three sports and, after scoring thirty-four points in his first game as a freshman power forward, a creative reporter with the school paper took his big night, and his royal name, and tabbed him "King Henry." The name followed him through high school and through an athletic scholarship to a small, division two college. Henry dropped out after a severe knee injury in his sophomore year, but the name stuck. It changed over the years from "King Henry", to "The King", to just "King" or "Kinger". He could not remember the last time someone called him Henry.

Henry glanced at the clock directly above the abandoned information center. 4:01 a.m.

"No, Jamal. I'm gonna chill down here tonight. Think I'll take my lunch outside and watch the stars. Later man." he said into the radio.

Henry pushed the janitor's cart into a corner by the front door. He pulled a dented, black lunch box from the bottom of the cart and stepped outside. It was a beautiful summer night. A warm breeze blew through the plaza as Henry walked to one of the white benches surrounding the massive flower pots. He picked his normal spot, giving him an unobstructed view of the night sky rising above the buildings to the south. Henry stretched his long legs and leaned back. He loved to sit and look up at the stars and wonder what might be up there so far away. Henry opened the rounded top to his metal lunch box. He smiled. On top of his usual sandwich, bag of chips and apple, Jeanie had placed a pack of Hostess cupcakes. For years now, ever since his minor heart attack, his wife kept him on a pretty strict diet, but every now and then she surprised him with a treat. As he unscrewed the top of his thermos, Henry noticed two uniformed police officers talking to two men in street clothes, at the far corner of the plaza. It seemed odd. Not many people inhabited Rockefeller Center in the wee hours of the morning, least of all cops. Henry stood and turned slowly in a complete circle, watching as he did. At least ten cops in suits and in uniform were within his sight. Henry shrugged his shoulders and sat back down to eat his lunch. Something was up, but it did not concern him. He un-wrapped the foil holding his baloney sandwich and placed them both on the bench. Next he emptied the bag of chips on the foil. The strong aroma of coffee wafted through his senses as he poured the steaming liquid into the metal cup. No matter what time of year, Henry needed his caffeine jolt to get him through the night. He lifted the cup to his lips.

The bullet hit him with a dull thud. He heard the thud, but felt no pain. He looked down at the small hole between his left pocket and the buttons on his shirt. Henry held onto the cupcake in his left hand, but dropped the metal cup from his right hand as the blood poured from the hole in his heart.

The sound of the metal cup bouncing off the stone plaza, startled the two officers closest to the bench where the dead janitor slumped. They assumed the man had fallen asleep.

Yet, they never questioned why the noise did not awaken the sleeping man.

Michael Muller did not wait to see if anyone reacted to the sharp pop created by the full metal jacket 308 Caliber Bullet as it left the silencer and broke the sound barrier on its way to its target. From the moment he squeezed the trigger and saw the impact through the scope, he was on the move. He unscrewed the silencer from the 86SR Mauser, quickly broke the high powered rifle down and packed it in his duffel bag. Minutes later, he was making his way down the thirty-seven floors of the office building by way of the back stairwell. Once in the parking garage, he climbed into the back of his rental van to wait. In the morning, at the height of rush hour, he would leave the building and disappear into traffic. Michael Mueller made himself comfortable. He could use a good night's sleep.

GAME 8

August 6th

"Your opponent is a person with a finite mind, a finite intellect and character weaknesses, who is trying to cover a situation that cannot be completely covered in the allotted time."

Shelby Lyman

P aul Worton stood in the same spot, in the same conference room where Officer Nicky Walsh first mentioned that the graphs on the wall might represent a game of chess. The room itself now served as headquarters for "The Chess Game Killer" investigation. Ten graphs now lined the conference room walls. The first seven graphs were littered with pictures, markings and written notes pertaining to Michael Mueller's two attempted murders and five victims. Worton's investigative task force spent close to twenty hours a day in the room pouring over every aspect of the case, trying to find any bit of information that might give them a clue to Mueller's next move. Every report from each crime scene was scrutinized over and over. Officers were assigned to every aspect of Mueller's life and every bit of information collected about him. Experts continued to review transcripts of Andy Wiley's computer messages and Worton's cell phone conversations with Mueller. And yet, the overwhelming concern of every member of the task force was to find the next location and victim.

Worton stared at the pictures of Rockefeller Center. The wide view of the plaza centered on a man, head slumped on his chest sitting on a white bench. The close up photo showed Henry Windsor's open eyes and shocked expression. Worton's stomach knotted. It was a helpless feeling knowing Michael Mueller would kill again in two days. He glanced at the three unmarked graphs remaining on the wall.

"Who and where?" he thought. "Who and where?"

Worton was distracted by the scratchy voice of "the Nuge".

"Are you sure that is exactly what he said?"

His good buddy, Bob Nugent, had spent a good part of every day in the conference room since Paul asked him to help out. "The Nuge" seemed out of place at first and some of the police experts might have considered him a nuisance. But Robert Nugent had a way of growing on people. In the month that the investigation had been open, "The Nuge" lifted spirits every time he shuffled into the overstaffed conference room. On top of that, every member of the task force had come to value his opinion. Now he was bent over a sheet of paper with a tech expert, working on the cell phone records of Mueller's calls to Worton.

"Yes Sir. That is what Detective Worton gave us," the officer said.

"Don't call me Sir, kid, it makes me feel old." "The Nuge" said.

"Hey Paul!" He yelled, not realizing that Paul Worton was now standing next to him.

"I'm right here, Nuge. What have you got?"

"Well, remember when you were at Rockefeller Center on the 2nd and Mueller called your cell phone?"

"Yeah, I remember. Why?"

"There is a quote here from Mueller that seems out of place with everything else we have from him. He says. *It is good to see a man proud of the place where he lives and wants to protect it and I am sure the place you live is proud of you.* First, it just seems like weird wording, and yet, I know I have seen a quote like this somewhere. I think he may be leaving another clue."

Worton did not hesitate. He spoke directly to the officer working with "The Nuge."

"Okay Mike, let's see if we can get this transcript to every available researcher. We need to find this quote. It has to have something to do with his next victim. It is August 5th. We only have about thirty-six hours."

Robert Nugent had moved to the wall of graphs. He stopped at the one marked #8, August 6th. He slowly ran his finger down a list of possible murder sights that investigators pinpointed in the ten block area between 106th Street and 96th Street. Suddenly his finger stopped.

"Of course!" He shouted. Every person in the room stopped to watch "The Nuge" pointing his arthritic middle finger, which stuck out all the time giving the impression that he was constantly flipping people off, at a point half way down the list on the wall.

"It's Lincoln. I knew I knew it. It was Lincoln all along." He said slapping his leg for emphasis.

"Calm down Nuge. What have you got? You mean Abe Lincoln? What about him?" Worton asked.

"They are his words. Lincoln's words. It is engraved on the wall inside the front entrance of The Museum of The City of New York. Proud of your city and your city is proud of you. It isn't exact, but it is the same quote." He turned and banged his finger on the wall. "The Museum is right here in the middle of 103rd and 5th Avenue. Right in the middle of our ten block area."

Paul Worton couldn't help but laugh. His friend looked like he would burst. His white hair was sticking out and he was red faced and out of breath.

"Great work, Nuge. Now sit down before you fall down. All right, the rest of us need to get on this. I want the Lincoln quote matched with Mueller's quote and I want people at the Museum now! I will call Copeland. If Nuge is right about this, the boss will want that place closed down before midnight and every person remotely connected with it out of there. Mueller is not going to win this one. Nicky, Jose and I will be at the museum if you find anything."

Worton walked toward the door and hit the speed dial on his cell phone.

"Hey Boss. Worton here. We found tomorrow's site."

* * *

"SWEET ANNIE'S" five female employees loved working for Lori Worton. Lori ran her business as if she was at a slumber party with her high school friends. Dress was casual at "SWEET ANNIE'S" and the coffee pot was always full. Laughter and girl talk were the order of the day and it was a rare day that someone didn't bring edible goodies for the whole crew to snack on. But today was different. Lori's morning greeting and patented smile were forced. Soon after the store opened, she claimed backed up paper work as an excuse to retreat to her office.

Lori sat at her desk staring at the time cards stacked in front of her. She could not get the daily headlines out of her head. As each day passed, and Michael Mueller stayed at large, the pressure mounted on her husband. This case was different than anything either of them had encountered before. There were actual dates where a known murder was about to take place and the whole city knew it was coming. Just not who or exactly where and all eyes were on Paul. To Lori the outcome seemed obvious. This so-called game would come down to the final date and her husband would be waiting for serial killer Michael Mueller to come to him. The thought terrified her. She knew Paul would not let Mueller carry out his vendetta on Grandmaster Victor Menchenko. She also knew her husband was dealing with a brilliant and vicious killer.

Her thoughts shifted to her daughter. Jackie watched the news and saw the headlines. Every day she heard from classmates about "The Chess Board Killer". They all wanted to know details that she did not know and they wanted to know when her dad was going to catch the guy. Lori did not know a happier, more outgoing kid than her daughter, but everything was wearing on her. Lately, she complained about everything from too much homework, to the length of softball practice, to arguments with her friends, to her chores. This morning they had argued again. Jackie was well aware of the rules for appropriate attire for school. When she showed up for breakfast wearing a mini-skirt and tank top, the problems had started. By the time Jackie had eaten, changed clothes, and slammed the front door on her way out, they were not speaking.

Lori looked up as the door opened after a soft knock. Melanie stuck her head in.

Melanie was her right hand man, so to speak. She had been at "SWEET ANNIE'S" the longest and knew the inventory as well as Lori did.

"Sorry to bug you, but do you have a minute?" She asked.

"Yeah. What's up Mel?"

"We have a foreign gentleman out here. I think he might be from Germany or something like that. Anyway, he purchased three antique pieces from out front and he wants to know if we can hold them for shipping until he returns to Europe in about three weeks?" Melanie explained.

"Sure. But why the wait?"

"Well. He said he lives alone and no one would be home to sign for them until he returns."

"That makes sense. No problem. We can ship whenever he wants." Lori said.

"Ok. He said he would come back or call to tell us the exact date to ship." Melanie said.

She started for the door and then hesitated.

"Listen Lori. I know things are really tense right now with all Paul is dealing with, and stuff with the store and everything. If you need to talk to someone you can bend my ear anytime, maybe over a drink after work or something?"

153

Lori smiled at her good friend.

"I didn't know it showed that much. Thanks for the offer, but I have to run today. Jackie has a game and I am already on her shit list. She has been a bear ever since her dad caught this case. I know she's just worried, but it has been tough. I'll take a rain check though."

"No problem. Just say the word." Melanie said, closing the door behind her.

Lori stared at the door for a long time. Finally, she picked up her pen and went back to work.

* * *

Andy Wiley was deep in thought as he took the subway steps two at a time before reaching the street level above. He was recognized everywhere now and had been accosted with various questions at least six times on his trip uptown. He was almost sick of the notoriety. He actually found himself empathizing with celebrities complaining about the paparazzi. "Almost sick of it" being the key phrase. He ignored most of the calls and e-mails he received each day, but not all of them. Agents, publishers and television executives needed to be weeded out. He would stay in contact with those most interested in a future book or movie about "The Chess Board Killer".

He now appeared on morning and evening news shows on a weekly basis, with the latest details about the most famous serial killer in the history of New York City. His column in *The Daily News* had newspaper sales soaring, as his stock rose across the country. Gigs on Larry King and Geraldo were already on the books and contracts were waiting to be signed for late night TV and Oprah.

He was still worried about his murderous news source, but sensed he was in no danger. He was convinced that this maniac only wanted publicity from him and he was more than happy to supply it. He wondered why the police had backed off. First, they threatened him with jail time. Then they asked for his help. Then they stopped talking to him. He wondered what that meant, as he unlocked his apartment door.

Andy Wiley dropped his knapsack on the floor and his computer bag on the couch. He strode across the apartment and sat at his desktop.

The small "**click me**" sign blinked on and off in the lower left hand corner of the screen.

* * *

The Museum of The City of New York looks like a museum. Its pale gray, stone facade sits back and above two flights of steps leading to a manicured courtyard flanked by columned patios. Inside the revolving front door, the museum gives off a quaint sense of historical clutter. Century old books and pictures give patrons a sense of New York City's great history and tradition.

Paul Worton stood just inside, to the left of the main entrance. He read the quote carved in the white marble wall for the tenth time.

**I LIKE TO SEE
A MAN PROUD
OF THE PLACE
IN WHICH HE
LIVES
I LIKE TO SEE
A MAN LIVE SO
THAT HIS PLACE
WILL BE PROUD
OF HIM
ABRAHAM LINCOLN**

"Nuge" was right: the words were not exact but it was definitely a clue from Mueller. Worton liked the quote. He did love the city, but he wasn't sure the city was too fond of him right now. Mueller and the Wiley kid from the *Daily News* had taken care of that. It was obvious the kid did not care. He was going to make a name for himself as long as Mueller fed him the info. As for Mueller, he was by far the toughest adversary Worton had ever encountered. He was brilliant, skilled and, obviously, extremely prepared. Yet he left different clues over and over again, not knowing if his opponent would figure out them, but not seeming to care if they did. This is what worried Worton the most. The man was extremely confident and he did not make mistakes. His thoughts were interrupted by Officer Morales.

"Ok Paul. We locked down the building at midnight last night and it will stay that way until midnight tonight. They will re-open at 8:00 a.m. tomorrow if we give the all clear." The detective said.

"Good! What about the canvas?" Worton said.

"Done. Every inch of this place, inside and out, has been checked. He is not here." Morales said, as Worton paced back and forth in front of him.

"Let's do it again. In fact, we probably need to do it every three hours until after midnight. Don't let anyone relax on this one. Understand Jose?"

"Got it, Paul." Morales said, as he walked away reaching for his radio.

Worton entered the gift shop to the left of Lincoln's quote. Crime Scene investigators were hard at work trying to find any small bit of evidence that might help. Worton approached the technician in charge.

"Willie, I want security tapes, receipts from the last month, and anything else you find, sent to forensics. We need some sort of break."

"You got it Detective." The man said without looking up.

* * *

The King's Gambit

On a bench in Central Park, directly across 5th Avenue from The Museum, hidden by trees and fences, Michael Mueller sat feeding a growing flock of pigeons. Occasionally, he paused to look through the high powered zoom lens on his 35 mm camera. He had watched the N.Y.P.D. descend on the city's historical archive at around 12:00 noon the day before. He had been surveying the building for close to an hour and was about to head for the entrance when the first patrol car arrived. He smiled. Always keep your fingers on a piece until you are absolutely positive of your move and its ramification.

That move could have killed him. Now he could regroup, give kudos to his opponent on another well played stalemate, and move on. Worton was very good at this and police officers were swarming all over his game board.

Mueller picked up his camera and bag and moved leisurely up 5th Avenue.

It was time to concentrate on game nine.

* * *

GAME 9
August 10th

When he reaches a point of demoralization a player can
crash, go to pieces, lose. Bobby Fischer says he waits for
the moment when his opponent's ego is crushed.
                                                      Shelby Lyman

The NYPD Swat Team from Emergency Services had been as discreet as possible cordoning off both ends of 64th Street and securing the alley behind the six story apartment building. Teams of four heavily armed men deployed in the lobby, stairwell and all exits were at the ready. Each man carried a Ruger mini-14 rifle, capable of firing a twenty round clip in seconds. Worton glanced at the twelve call box buttons just below a line of mailbox slots cut into a bronze rectangle on the wall. The name Frank Lewitzky was stenciled between the black button and the mailbox slot for apartment two on the second floor.

The Task Force had attacked the information gathered at The Museum with a vengeance. The security films gathered over the last month showed only one repeat male customer who came close to the size and make up they were looking for. He wore a baseball cap and stayed slump shouldered most of the time except the one instant he looked directly into the camera. When Worton saw the man in the frozen picture frame, he knew instantly he was looking into the eyes of Michael Mueller. They now had a new name, fingerprints, credit card receipts, an address and maybe a face.

The man had entered the museum on July 20th and again on August 1st. Each time he paid for items in the gift shop with a credit card and each time the name Frank Lewitzky came up. Fingerprints were taken from the receipts and forensics took three days to match Michael Mueller's handwriting with that of Frank Lewitzky. They were one and the same man. It was soon evident why they had not found any information on Michael Mueller once he left his Sag Harbor home. He was living a second life in the City as Frank Lewitzky. Bank accounts, credit card accounts, voter registration cards and driver's license records, all led to the same address on the Upper West Side of Manhattan.

The Task Force was about to make a visit to Frank Lewitzky—aka---Michael Mueller. Worton drew his weapon from the shoulder holster and then spoke into his hand held radio.

"Okay Lieutenant, are your guys ready?" The voice of the ESU officer in charge crackled in his ear as they started up the stairwell.

"Let's do this." He barked.

Worton could not get one thought out of his mind: was this Mueller's second mistake or just another clue in his twisted game.

* * *

Jackie Worton sat at the back of the bus, alone. Her friends chose to stay clear of her these days, with good reason. She knew she had been a bitch for a while now.

Over her headphones she heard laughter and glanced toward the front. Her best friends in the world, Karen, Milly and Janice, were in hysterics over something. She felt a pang of jealousy. Jackie caught Karen's eye, and the girl's smile faded immediately. Karen quickly looked away. Jackie Worton squeezed her eyes shut tightly, stifling a scream. God, what is wrong with me. Now, I'm making my friends feel guilty for having fun. Not to mention making my mom's life miserable.

That morning she had deliberately provoked a fight. She left the house mad at her mom and mad at the world. Now she found herself sitting alone, feeling sorry for herself. She reached inside her blouse and fingered the ring at the end of the gold chain. Yeah, she missed her dad and she was worried sick that something bad would happen to him, but her friends were not to blame. They were only trying to help, and her mom was the best mom in the world. She had to be even more worried than Jackie was about her dad. No parents she knew were more in love than her mom and dad. Much to her embarrassment, they acted like love-starved teenagers around her friends.

Jackie felt tears of anger in her eyes. Damn it. He would expect more of me. She would fix things with her mom tonight.

The bus stopped for a pickup and she moved up the isle toward her friends. Jackie fingered the ring and whispered,

"Please take care of him"

"Hey guys! What is so funny? She asked with as big a smile as she could muster, while sliding into the seat next to Karen.

* * *

Michael Mueller flopped on the queen-sized bed in the two-room flat he had just rented across the river in New Jersey. He had paid a month's rent in advance. He needed a place to eat, sleep, work and not be bothered. He paid with cash and the landlord assured him that he would be left alone. His adrenaline was at its peak on a daily basis now and he had to use his breathing exercises to control his heart rate, to keep him focused and to keep him level headed.

Two games left. He had to be careful. He was pretty sure Worton would center his attention on Penn Station. But defending it would be a monumental task. He must not underestimate his opponent again. Worton had proved to be uncanny and crafty.

All his plans. All his dreams. All his vindication would come down to the last game. He just had to get there. He could not make a blunder now.

It was time to contact Mr. Wiley one last time. His choice of a media dupe had been brilliant. Wiley's coverage could not have been more thorough or sensational. Michael Mueller smiled as he started typing on his lap top.

Of course, Andy Wiley had no clue of what his involvement really was.

* * *

The apartment was empty. The swat team quickly cleared the four rooms and Crime Scene took over. Before they could start, the detectives stationed themselves in separate rooms to observe and take notes, Morales in the kitchen, Nicky Walsh in the bedroom and Worton in the living room/dining room area.

For two hours, Nicky Walsh made her way around the bedroom and master bath, maneuvering to stay out of forensics' way as they went about the business of collecting evidence. Now she stood in the far left corner of the room from the doorway, between the wall and the window. The bedding had been stripped and bagged, and the headboard was being pulled away from the wall, when something caught her eye. Maybe a change in the light or a shadow, but something made her move closer to the corner and look down the wall. The crease in the wallpaper looked deeper, or was the paper just mis-matched? Nicky moved closer and ran her hand down the seam, feeling a ridge. Her stomach fluttered as she looked around, not exactly sure for what, but there was a distinct crack in the wall from ceiling to floor, and it was not there by accident. Suddenly, she saw it. A red button about two feet up from the floor was hidden by the floral wallpaper design.

She bent to a squat and tentatively pressed the button.

"Hey guys! You might want to see this?" she yelled out.

When Worton entered the room, Nicky Walsh had her service weapon out, trained on the wall in front of her, as it slid to her left, disappearing and revealing a six foot ceiling to floor opening.

"Crime Scene out," he barked. "Nicky back away from the opening but keep that door covered." Worton had his own weapon trained on the opening now, and his radio in his other hand. He spoke into it.

"Swat, we need backup in the master bedroom now!"

* * *

Tim Copeland sat back in his swivel chair clasping his hands behind his head. The room was dark, except for the glow of the flat screen TV on top of the file cabinet in the corner. He had just hung up from a conference call involving every big wig in the department. They were losing patience. The Governor's office, the Mayor's office and the media were exerting tremendous pressure on his bosses to have Worton removed as lead detective on "The Chess Board Murder" case. He would not budge. It might mean his job in the long run, but if they were going to catch this guy, he didn't have a better man than Worton, especially not at this late date. They were close. He knew it. They had a second name to go on, and an address. Worton had called to say Mueller was not on the premises, but that a panic room had been found inside Lewitzky's apartment and he wanted Copeland to see it as soon as possible.

He would leave as soon as he finished watching Andy Wiley's exclusive report on New York's at-large serial killer.

* * *

The King's Gambit

Andy Wiley took his cue from the set director and looked into the camera.

"There have now been five murders and three attempted murders in "The Chess Board Murder" case. One Michael Mueller, a blackjack dealer from Sag Harbor and former chess protégé of world renowned chess Grandmaster Victor Menchenko, has created an insane chess match against the New York City Police department. He has killed five men whom he anointed "Kings" in his own twisted fantasy. They are Vincent Antonelli, "King" of the Philharmonic in Carnegie Hall; Jorge Gonzales, "King" of the L.I.R.R. Teamsters in Union Square; Professor Clifton Davenport, "King" of academics at The American Academy of Dramatic Arts; Officer Anthony Austin, "King" of athletes at The Police Academy Training Center, and Henry Windsor or "King Henry", former star athlete here in New York City. His other intended victims included a drug kingpin in Spanish Harlem, a crown-wearing tour guide at The Guggenheim and a curator at The Museum of The City of New York, who happened to be named David "King". Wiley stared into the camera for effect.

"Michael Mueller has no emotional attachment to any of his victims. He simply considers them pawns in a deadly game of life and death on the chess board of New York City. He has two more games left to play, August 10th and then again on August 31st. It will be the last time we will hear from this serial killer. The question is, will he complete his mission of beating the finest police department in the world in this bizarre chess match, or will he be caught. One thing is certain, win or lose Michael Mueller will be remembered forever because of the terror he created in the summer of the "Chess Board" killings.

Copeland switched off the TV and grabbed his keys. Wiley was right. Mueller had already succeeded. No one would ever talk about the game of chess again without mentioning the killer's name and what he had done. As he left his office, Copeland hoped they would remember the bastard as dead or rotting in jail.

Paul Worton would not let Crime Scene do their thing in Michael Mueller's recently discovered hidden room until Nicky Walsh could document everything she saw and Detective Morales finished taking pictures from every angle. He also wanted Tim Copeland to see the room the way they found it.

He stood in the center of the room, in front of a wooden high backed stool pushed up under a large slanted easel. He glanced around the room, starting with a huge poster of Bobby Fischer staring down at him from the wall directly across the room. He watched Officer Walsh open each of ten lockers lined along the far left wall. Each one contained a change of clothing and a knapsack. Next to the lockers a list of names appeared on a chart pinned to the wall.

DETECTIVE PAUL WORTON/SPASSKY
212-376-1554 CELL PHONE
DETECTIVE TIM COPELAND
DETECTIVE JOSE MORALES
DETECTIVE ANTHONY AUSTIN: deceased
OFFICER NICOLE WALSH
ANDREW WILEY/ MEDIA

Directly in front of him, a large map of New York City adorned the wall next to Fischer's picture. Each murder site, numbered one through ten, was circled in red. One through eight had a red arrow drawn out to the margin. Written in magic marker on the wall, at the end of each arrow, was a notation. Each notation listed a name, a place and an outcome. Number one read;

VINCENT ANTONELLI, CARNIGIE HALL---WIN

Five locations had the word WIN listed. The other three, the park in Spanish Harlem, the Guggenheim Museum and the Museum of The City of New York, had the word STALEMATE at the end of each notation. The last two circled sites had names and locations but no outcome listed.

Worton focused on the last two sites.

#9----MADISON SQUARE GARDEN AUGUST 10th---KING OF COOL

#10---TRACY TOWERS/ 2nd AVENUE & 24th STREET MENCHENKO

He was trying to take it all in when Tim Copeland stepped into the room. He was wearing the obligatory white booties on his shoes and pulling on a pair of plastic gloves as he entered.

"Wow! I guess we found his lair. If that's what you want to call it," he said.

"Yeah, it looks like we actually had him pegged pretty well. Hopefully, there is something here that will help us catch him." Worton said. "According to that map, we were right about Menchenko. He is Mueller's last target, the guy he really wants. But maybe it never goes that far. Maybe we catch him at Madison Square Garden."

Copeland nodded his head as he studied the map.

"When do we get forensics in here so they can get started?"

Worton pointed to the top of the easel. Two plastic baggies were taped to the surface. Inside each appeared to be a folded piece of paper.

"You know the paper grids he left on each victim? Well, I am assuming these two pieces of paper pertain to the last two murder sites. I want to open them, and I wanted you here before I did."

"Let's do it." Copeland said.

Worton opened the baggy taped below the number nine and unfolded the piece of paper.

"It matches Madison Square Garden." He said, then repeated the process for number ten.

"Looks like Tracy Towers. Menchenko's apartment building."

"Ok. Lock this place down." Copeland said." As far as I can tell, he will be coming back here unless he figures out that we found the place. Put some of our people in the adjacent buildings. I want our people inconspicuous, but alert. I will get authorization to do what we need. It won't be hard. The big wigs are in a frenzy to end this. Let's get forensics in here and find out who the "King Of Cool" is."

He took one more look around the room before turning and leaving.

"Man what a psycho."

"Jose! Nicky! How we doing? We need to get forensics in here." Worton said.

A few minutes later, as crime scene investigators began their work, he noticed for the first time a pair of rubber gloves hanging from a hook on the edge of the table.

"Why would Mueller wear rubber gloves in a place he never expected us to find?" he whispered to himself.

* * *

GAME 10
September 1st

"The End Game is the equivalent of sudden death at all times."
Shelby Lyman

August 11th dropped on New York City and surrounding areas like a steaming hot face towel at a neighborhood barbershop. The entire northeastern seaboard had been sweltering for over a month, and today was no different. By 8:00 a.m. the temperature was already eighty-five degrees and the humidity was stifling. Paul Worton sat glistening in a sheen of his own sweat. He had left the comfort of his air conditioned house thirty minutes earlier, sat on the top porch step and had not moved since. The sweat soaked his t-shirt. His arms and legs were wet, and drops fell from his nose. He blinked to squeeze the salty liquid from his eyes. He had nothing to do for the next twenty days except wait to confront Michael Mueller in person.

The last five days had seemed like an eternity. They now knew that Frank Lewitzky was nothing but an alias. A name for Mueller to use if the police uncovered his identity, which they did when they found his fingerprints on the remote control unit used to lure little Miguel Vargas into the street a month earlier. The rubber gloves found in the panic room had Michael Mueller's fingerprints etched into the tips. Every other print found in the apartment was a smudged deformity of a print. Experts determined that Mueller had in all probability burnt his fingertips, probably with acid, in order to destroy all evidence of his original prints. He had covered his tracks. The plan was simple if and when Worton and his crew went looking for Michael Mueller, he would take on the identity of Frank Lewitzky.

The evidence found at the apartment showed two things. First: Mueller was fixated on exacting revenge on Victor Menchenko on September 1st, and someone referred to as the "King of Cool" would be a target somewhere around Madison Square Garden on August 10th. The folded paper had a grid which encompassed Menchenko's address within the kill zone. His name and address were written on the wall next to the map. A scrapbook of newspaper clippings, dating back to Mueller's years with Menchenko was stuffed with articles marking the career and accolades of the great Grand Master, and a quote written on the back wall of the panic room showed the killer's fixation with his former tutor. The quote read.

"No, Michael. You will never be good enough."
Victor Menchenko

Worton refused to dwell on Menchenko and August 31st. He had a more pressing problem. He had to find the latest target somewhere around Madison Square Garden before Mueller could execute him on August 10th.

He sent his people on a frantic search to find the "King of Cool" before it was too late. They descended on Penn Station and Madison Square Garden on the 10th looking for any sign that might lead them to the killer or the victim. Back at the station house, the task force checked every employment record of the businesses in the Penn Station terminal. Every person listed on the Long Island Railroad payroll, every team roster and every act scheduled to perform at The Garden was also under scrutiny. They found hundreds of possibilities, and attempted to protect them all. But they failed.

Worton wiped the sweat from his face. He leaned forward with his elbows on his knees.

The investigators saw the obvious as soon as they got the list of businesses in or around Madison Square Garden and Penn Station. They were looking for "The King Of Cool" and *Smoothie King* sells ice cream at Penn Station. It is a small business situated to the right of a bank of escalators that leads travelers to the trains. But they were too late. The Task Force arrived just as the morning manager pulled back the iron gate on the morning of August 10th and flipped on the neon lights to the

"SMOOTHIE KING"

Within minutes, the task force descended on the store and shut it down. Quickly a search of the facility was underway and a list of workers produced. Everyone was accounted for, except the store manager. Martin Burns was not expected at work that day. Calls to his cell phone went unanswered and officers were dispatched to his house. He could not be found.

That is until a scream ripped through the tiny soda fountain.

A young, female assistant manager was showing officers the back of the store, the kitchen, the supply room and the walk-in freezer. When they opened the freezer door, the cold dead eyes of Martin Burns stared back at them. He was standing on tiptoes, with his hands tied over each side of a ceiling pipe. He was gagged, with a blue frost covering his hair, eyebrows and face.

The face haunted Worton as he sat in the morning heat.

The Task Force was still hard at work. "The Nuge" was basically living at the precinct. Detective Morales and Nicky Walsh had joined him.

Copeland was still fighting with City Hall.

His daughter was so worried about him that she could hardly talk to him without crying, and Lori had actually asked him to resign from the case.

Menchenko was holed up in his apartment, basically under 'round the clock, house arrest.

But Worton was waiting. Waiting for August 31st. Waiting to meet Michael Mueller.

He was also waiting for the call he knew was coming.

As if on cue, the ringer sounded on his cell phone. He pushed the tape recorder "on" button and picked up his phone.

"Worton here."

"Detective! It has been quite a while since we last spoke. We have both been very busy." Mueller said.

Worton did not answer.

"You continue to astound me, Detective. I never thought you would find the apartment. How did you manage that? You know, if I had not been returning there right when your swat teams were surrounding the back entrance, I might have walked right into a trap. It took all I could do to calm down and keep walking."

"Should I call you Michael or Frank?" Worton asked.

"Well, I knew from the start, if you were any good, I would need a second identity. But I must admit, I did not think I would need a third." Mueller said.

"Sorry to inconvenience you."

"Can you believe how hot it is Detective? At least for most of us, but not for poor Mister Burns."

"It is not enough that you kill innocent people, you feel the need to ridicule them too?"

"You are right Detective, my apologies. You know, over the last four games you have discovered all four sites and thwarted me twice, causing two stalemates. You also found my apartment making the last two games much harder for me to win. I had to change a lot of plans and find a new home base. Although I do admit, finding the trapped "King" at Penn Station or my Rockefeller Center target was a tall task to say the least. But that is what happens in classic chess games. When great players present various attacks, the defender is in great peril."

"Except this is no chess game."

"Semantics, Detective. All over the country people are watching us, thanks to the fine work of the new media darling, Mister Andy Wiley. The world will always use chess terms when speaking of our encounter." Mueller said.

"What now Mueller?"

"Now I must go and start to prepare. This will be the culmination of my work. This will have to be my most beautiful move. You know my target. You know his location. It will be a monumental task, but I will be ready." Mueller paused for a moment. "Detective, I must tell you, from the very beginning of our match you have been such a worthy opponent. Your moves have been most beautiful in their own right. I hate for it to end, but end it must. You will not hear from me again before our final meeting Detective. My hope is that I will be remembered for a long time to come, especially by you."

The line went dead. Worton shut off the tape and snapped the phone shut.

"I will be there." He whispered.

* * *

By August 31st the humidity had broken some, but the temperature was still in the eighties at 6:00 p.m. Paul stood in the center of his master bedroom. He snapped his holster to his belt and clipped his badge to the inside pocket of his suit jacket. Standard issue weapons for a New York City police officer can include the Sig Sauser 226- 9mm, the Smith Wesson 5946-9mm, or the Glock 19-9mm. But Worton was old school when it came to weapons and none of these guns fit his needs. He liked the feel of his Smith & Wesson .38 special revolver, as he slipped it in his holster. He then made sure his back-up was loaded and secure before strapping it to his ankle. He picked up his jacket, took a deep breath and headed downstairs. He knew they would be waiting.

* * *

Lori leaned against the kitchen counter, just to the right of the stainless steel double sink, sipping on an oversized mug of coffee. Her daughter sat on the opposite side of the counter. Jackie used her fork to aimlessly push the macaroni and cheese across her plate. She did not look up when her father entered the room. Paul poured coffee into his travel cup. He looked from Lori to Jackie, and back again. Finally he spoke.

"So, big game tomorrow Kiddo?"

"I'm not going." Jackie said, without looking up.

"What are you talking about? Your team is counting on you."

"I'm staying home with Mom." She mumbled. .

"Honey, I'm going to the store tomorrow." Lori said.

"Then I'm going with you,"

Paul started to try to reason with his daughter but before he could even start, she jumped from her seat throwing her arms around his waist, burying her head in his chest.

"I'm so scared that he is going to hurt you." She sobbed.

"Hey easy, easy he doesn't want me. He wants his old teacher, and he will never even get close to the room I am in. The whole building is covered and has been for days. This will all be over in about thirty hours and I will wake you when I get home."

"You promise?" She sniffed. He took her by the chin and tilted her head up.

"Have I ever lied to you?" He asked, with his most reassuring smile.

"No." She said, wiping away a tear.

"I expect to hear about a couple of hits and a shutout when I get home."

"I can't promise a shutout, but I will try."

"What are you going to do the rest of the day?"

"Get some sun and read. I have one more book to finish for my summer reading, *To Kill a Mockingbird.*

"Ah! Atticus Finch, Scout, Boo Radley. One of my all-time favorites. You know, it is one of the few movies made that is almost as good as the book itself. We should watch it together sometime."

"I would like that Dad." She beamed.

"Ok. Beat it. Let me talk to your mom".

"Promise to wake me?"

"You know I will."

Jackie bounced out of the room with a smile on her face.

"It never ceases to amaze me how you're able to talk to her and make everything sound okay." Lori said, shaking her head.

"It is all true," Paul said. "This guy wants Menchenko, not me. The guys will scoop him up before he ever gets close to me."

Lori's eyes flashed anger for a moment.

"Don't try to con me, Paul! I know the job and I know it is never foolproof. There are no guarantees and you know it. I also know you have never had to face a perp like Mueller and I know how dangerous he is. The worst part is, I know you. The only way he gets to Menchenko is through you." She paused and looked in his eyes. "Tell me I'm wrong."

"What do you want me to do, Lori? He has killed six people. He killed Anthony. I'm not letting him get away. I will stop him."

Lori stepped to him, putting her arms around his neck. She kissed him as long and deeply as she ever had. She stepped back fighting her tears.

"Promise that you will not take chances. Promise that you will be careful. Promise that you will come back to us."

Paul Worton looked at the only woman he ever loved.

"I promise I will come home to you." He turned, grabbed his keys from the peg board, and walked out the door.

Lori leaned back against the counter, head down and arms folded.

"Please!" she whispered.

* * *

Officer Nicky Walsh and Detective Jose Morales walked into the Task Force conference room located on the sixth floor of the 18th Precinct at 7:00 a.m. The room was empty except for Robert Nugent and three Crime Lab specialists. Detective Morales spent the first four hours of September 1st in Victor Menchenko's apartment with the Grandmaster and Paul Worton. Finally, Worton sent Morales to get Officer Walsh and head back to the station house. He was not satisfied. Even though they knew the location and the target, Worton wanted round the clock work done, digging through everything they had on the "Chess Board Murders". He was looking for any piece of evidence or clue that Mueller might have left. The question remained, how did he plan to get to Menchenko? Nothing could be left to chance.

Nicky Walsh was talking to the other officers in the room when Morales approached "The Nuge".

"Hey Nuge, anything new?" He said. Nuge answered without looking up at Morales.

"Hello Jo-Jo have you been with Paul and Menchenko?" The Nuge had taken to calling the Spanish-American detective Jo Jo.

"Yeah, nothing happening there, but everyone is on edge. Maybe that's all he wants: to make us crazy. He must know he can't get to him." Morales said.

"Don't kid yourself, Jo-Jo. He plans to end this tonight. Somehow he thinks he can get to Menchenko and get away without being caught."

"I know, but Tracy Towers is like Fort Knox right now and even if he could get to him, Paul's sitting right there in the same room. I don't know how he can get it done and get out."

Nuge continued to stare at the grid of New York City on the wall.

	8th Ave.	7th Ave.	6th Ave.	5th Ave.	4th Ave.	3rd Ave.	2nd Ave.
9th Ave. 96th St.				5th Ave. Museum of The City of New York			2nd Ave. Spanish Harlem
86th St.				The Guggenheim Museum			
72nd St.							
57th St.		Carnegie Hall					
42nd St.			Rockefeller Center				
34th St.						The Daily News	
23rd St.	Penn Station			American Academy of Performing Arts		Tracy Towers	
9th Ave. 14th St.	8th Ave.	7th Ave.	6th Ave Union Station	5th Ave.	4th Ave.	3rd Ave. Police Academy	2nd Ave

"Exactly." He said.

* * *

Andy Wiley walked through the deserted lobby of the *Daily News* building at exactly 11:45 p.m. The main lobby would not open again until 8:00 a.m. but he had used his master key to get in the front entrance. He did not want anyone to know he was in the building. His heels clicked on the marble floors as the echoes bounced off the stone walls. He did not look at the line of over-sized clocks on the left hand wall, each one depicting a different time zone. Bronze plaques located below stated the given country that coincided with each clock. He did not look at the one focal point of the *Daily News* building that catches the eye of each person as they enter the lobby. A mammoth globe is situated in the center of the lobby. The top half of the globe rises from the floor and is surrounded by bronze railings for tourists and visitors to look down on the rotating earth.

Head down, Andy Wiley strode straight to the elevators. He had to get to his office before midnight. Michael Mueller's last communiqué instructed him to be in his office at 12:01 a.m. September 1st. He was to wait for further instructions. This would be a first. Mueller had never contacted him except through his home computer. Mueller made it clear this would be the final "Game" in his chess match with the New York City Police Department. He also made it clear that Wiley needed to be in his office if he wanted an exclusive report that would make him a legend in the news business. He would be able to pick his spots for the rest of his career. A book would be a definite, and movie rights a distinct possibility. All he had to do was go to his office, get his instructions and wait.

The elevator stopped at the fourth floor. Wiley unlocked his office, flicked on the lights and went straight to his computer. In the bottom left hand corner the words "be patient" flashed on and off.

He sat at his desk to wait.

"Man, this guy is something." He thought.

* * *

Michael Mueller glanced at the clock on the dressing table. *9:45AM* He was excited. The adrenaline was at a high. He used his breathing exercises to calm his emotions. Today he needed to be at his best. Nothing left to chance: everything done in a deliberate, calm mode. He pulled a skin-tight t-shirt over his head that matched the jogging pants he was already wearing. He then tied the laces to his Adidas running shoes, put on his baseball cap and sunglasses and checked himself in the mirror. He smiled to himself. Worton and Menchenko would have been waiting for him close to ten hours now.

Mueller picked up his hiking pack and left the room.

* * *

Paul Worton watched Victor Menchenko's long, thin fingers twirl the captured bishop in his hand. It was the tenth piece that Paul had lost in the half hour that they had been playing. Worton had asked for the game for various reasons as night turned to day, Menchenko had not slept a wink. He paced, drank coffee, smoked his pipe and asked Worton question after question about what might happen in the next twenty-four hours. He was way out of his comfort zone. He explained that he never meant any harm to the Mueller family. The boy just did not have what it took to be a World Champion. It would have been worse to string them along. He was trying to do them a favor. Finally, Worton stopped him. He pointed to an ornate ebony and ivory chess set on an antique side table.

"Shall we play?" Worton asked.

Menchenko stopped pacing.

"Do you play Detective?"

Worton smiled.

"Yes, on occasion, when my Dad or my friend, Nuge, talk me into it. But I never win, or I'm too impatient. This will be like my softball-playing daughter taking swings against Josh Beckett. But I thought if you were gentle, you could teach me a few things and we might ease the tension."

Two hours later, they were on game three and it had been ugly. Menchenko continued to twirl the black chess piece in his fingers while staring intently at the board.

"You know your next 5, 6, 10 moves, don't you?" Worton asked. Menchenko watched Worton for a moment.

"Yes, you have to play ahead of yourself in this game, especially against great players. You have to be prepared to change your tactics at any minute depending upon your opponent's moves or strategies," he said. "You are a good life player, Detective. You are not really concentrating on this game – you are studying me."

"More like, trying to get a handle on him through you." Worton said. "Explain to me about the 'End Game'."

"The 'End Game' in chess is when you see the end in sight and feel your opponent is at his most vulnerable. Your whole game has been planned to get to this point – to crush him."

"But isn't your opponent trying to do the same?"

"Yes, of course, and many games end in a stalemate for that very reason. You must be very careful because the 'End Game' you perceive could still have unexpected twists. You must be ready to react and change at all times. Really, the 'End Game' in a great match can be exhilarating." Menchenko had leaned forward and his eyes flashed as he spoke about the game he loved. Worton leaned back in his chair.

"Let's hope we're ready for whatever Mueller's next move might be." He said.

* * *

Lori Worton drove to work in the same bumper-to-bumper, 60 mph, four-lane traffic that permeated every Long Island rush hour. Her driving was robotic, using skills worn into her psyche from over twenty years of New York City driving. Her mind was not on the road or the cars in front of her. Luckily, nothing out of the ordinary happened. No accidents, no construction slow-downs, no early-morning idiot cutting her off to move up one car length. It was a good thing. Her thoughts were on her husband and her daughter. She wanted to be at work because if the worst happened, she would be notified there. If Paul was hurt, or worse, she would deal with the situation, and then go to Jackie. She and

Paul had convinced Jackie that everything would be fine. She would stay home, read her book, get some sun and go to her game. Lori would stay at work and wait. After she closed the store, if Paul had still not called, she would go to Jackie's game and wait. Paul promised to call her as soon as it was over. He said everything would be fine, but she knew the words were hollow. No one knew exactly what Michael Mueller was capable of.

Lori parked in her private owner's slot and walked toward the back entrance to "Sweet Annie's". She hoped it would be Paul's voice that she heard and not Tim Copeland's. If Copeland called, it meant that Paul was not capable of calling her.

* * *

"The Nuge" was restless. He had left his perch in front of the wall with the New York City grid printed on it. He was in the process of reviewing every note, every interview, every photo and every piece of evidence. He had a growing feeling that something was not right. Detective Morales and Nicky Walsh were helping. They took each item, scrutinized it, discussed it and labeled it as 'Checked on September 1st'. They were currently working on the phone transcripts between Mueller and Worton. "The Nuge" had suggested that hearing them might give them a different perspective and Nicky Walsh was reading them aloud.

Nuge's brow furrowed.

"Wait, go back and read that again." He said. Nicky flipped the page back and started reading Mueller's words again.

"'Now I must go and start to prepare. This will be the culmination of my work. This will be my most beautiful move.'" Nicky read from the transcript.

"Okay. Okay. Now skip down toward the end," Nuge said, sounding a little agitated. Nicky continued reading.

"'You know my target. You know his location. It will be a monumental task, but I will be ready. I must tell you Detective, from the very beginning of our match you have been such a worthy opponent. Your moves have been most beautiful in their own right.'" "The Nuge" interrupted her again.

"Right there, read that right there."

"Your moves have been most beautiful in their own right?" she asked.

"That doesn't sound right. That sounds weird, that same phrase in both sentences. 'My most beautiful move'. 'Your moves have been most beautiful.' Is it me, or does that sound strange?"

"I guess, a little," Morales said. "He usually just talks in chess speak, like he really is playing a game. The words, 'most beautiful, seems strange. What do you make of it?"

Nicky Walsh placed the transcript on the table and stood up. She was no longer listening to the two men.

"I don't know if it means anything," Nuge said. "But this guy loves to live on the edge, like leaving the grid chessboards, leaving the 'Cooler King' quote, leaving the fingerprints on the rubber gloves, playing on words. You know what I mean?"

Nicky's stomach was doing flip flops as she moved across the room.

"Where are those books on chess we had?" She asked. "There was a stack of them."

Nuge and Morales were watching her now as she turned, anxiously looking around the room.

"They are over in that corner," Nuge said. "Why?"

Nicky moved quickly to a stack of about twenty books piled on the floor in the corner. She knelt on one knee and quickly started pushing them aside until she found what she was looking for, a hard cover, 12 by 16 inch book. The cover read *"Chess: A Celebration of Two Thousand Years"*. She dropped the book on the table. Quickly, her hands flew through the pages, all the while mumbling "Most beautiful move... most beautiful move" and finally, she stopped.

"Oh my God!"

"What is it?" Morales asked.

"1912 World Championship Match known as "The Most Beautiful Move" in chess history." Nicky's hands were shaking as she spoke.

"It could be just a coincidence." He said, trying to convince himself.

Nicky spun the book around so they could read it.

"I don't think so," she said. "The match was between American Frank Marshall and Russian Stefan Lewitzky." The three stared at each other.

"Shit!" Morales said. "Frank Lewitzky. That's the alias Mueller's been using".

"Yeah, and in this game, he is after a Queen not a King." Nicky Walsh said.

* * *

Lori glanced at the clock on her desk. **5:30** She would have to leave soon in order to get to Jackie's game by eight-thirty. The store normally closed at seven-thirty during the summer but Melanie would take care of the closeout and lock up.

Six and a half hours until midnight and still no word from Paul. Her stomach tightened with each passing second. Jackie would want to know about her dad and Lori had no answers.

Melanie knocked on the door and poked her head in.

"Lori, remember the European guy that put some stuff on hold for shipment a few weeks ago?"

"Yeah, is he ready for shipment?" Lori asked.

"Well, yeah, but he asked to see his items set up before we packed them. So I did and now he wants to see the manager." Melanie said.

"Is there a problem with the stuff? Is something broken?"

"Not that I can see," Melanie said. "Maybe he's just a satisfied customer who wants to thank you in person."

"Okay, where is he?" Lori asked.

181

"He's waiting in the storeroom and I have another customer out front."

"Thanks. I'll handle it."

Lori entered the back storeroom. The man waiting was tall and very distinguished, with graying hair and sideburns. He was over six feet tall and dressed in an Armani suit. Lori placed him in his late sixties to early seventies.

"Hello. I'm Lori Worton, owner of "Sweet Annie's". How may I help you?"

The man answered in a thick European accent. "I just wanted to check on the items I had purchased. Two of the items are fine, but there seems to be a problem with the antique Civil War chess set." He said.

Lori walked to the table and studied the ornate silver and blue chess set. Her stomach turned and a cold sweat instantly washed over her. In the middle square sat her husband's State Championship ring. Her mind raced. She wanted to scream but did not. She tried to push all her emotions to the back of her mind.

"Where is my daughter?" She whispered.

"Let me assure you, she is safe," Michael Mueller answered. "She is unharmed but will be quite groggy when she awakes. When I found her, she was sunning in your back yard, reading a book and listening to music. The headphones helped. She didn't see me before she fell asleep. The aerosol spray is completely harmless. She will sleep for about ten hours." Mueller said.

"How do I know she is safe?"

"You will have to trust me. Let us assume you do nothing stupid. In a few hours she will awake and be no worse for the wear. If you do not cooperate, this store will close early. I will be long gone before anyone finds you or your co-workers, and no one will ever find your daughter. Now I need you to make an excuse to leave for the day. Then you will accompany me to see Mr. Andy Wiley at the *Daily News* building." Mueller said.

"If I do what you ask, Jackie will be okay?"

"I was with your daughter. If she was my target, she would be dead and I would be long gone. You just need to cooperate. Can you do that?"

"Yes." Lori answered.

"Okay. First, package these for shipping as you normally would," Mueller instructed. "Second, make up some excuse for leaving for the day. Do not jeopardize your daughter by doing something stupid. No calls, no text messages. Do you understand?"

"Yes."

Mueller watched Lori go through each task. When they stepped out of the storeroom, Lori was all business. She set the items near the checkout counter and started to complete the packing slips.

"I'm sure I've forgotten your name." She said, with a smile.

"Lewitzky. Mr. Frank Lewitzky." Mueller said.

"That's right. Will you be paying by check or credit card, Mr. Lewitzky?" Lori asked.

Mueller smiled as he reached into his jacket and pulled out a billfold.

"Credit." He said, as he handed her his credit card.

Lori wrote up the invoice and credit card slip. When the transaction was complete, Lori thanked him for his business.

"No, I'm quite grateful for your patience and cooperation." He said. "Perhaps I could buy you a drink or a cup of coffee before I go."

"Thank you for your offer but, in reality, I have to leave soon. My daughter is playing in an important softball game tonight and I promised I would be there."

"Well, maybe I could walk you out?" He said smiling.

"Okay, I just have to tell my staff." Lori called across the room.

"Hey, Mel, I'm leaving early. I've got to get to Jackie's game." Melanie looked puzzled.

"Okay, but I thought you wanted to be here when Paul called."

"He'll call my cell phone first, and I really feel like I need to be with Jackie tonight. I think maybe I'll take her and her friends to TERESA' S for ice cream on the way home from the game. They love that place and it should take her mind off her dad. I'm going to walk Mr. Lewitzky out. The paperwork for his shipment is right here." She said, putting the paperwork on the counter.

"Okay." Melanie called from the novelty section where she was stocking shelves. Michael Mueller stepped forward, close to Lori.

"May I look at the papers? It would be just like a detective's wife to leave some sort of clue".

Lori handed him the papers. "Good girl." He said, after a quick glance at the papers.

"Shall we go?"

Lori picked up her bag and keys, placed the invoice back on the desk and followed Michael Mueller from the store.

* * *

The great-grandfather clock struck 7:00 p.m. Only five hours to go. Paul Worton was on his fourth can of Starbuck's Double Shots. He needed the caffeine jolt, even though he could not have been more on edge. Mueller would not sit this one out, but Worton was uneasy. Had they guessed wrong?

His cell-phone rang and he glanced at the caller ID.

"Nuge. What's up?" He asked.

"Paul. Menchenko is not his target."

Worton squeezed his eyes tightly shut. His stomach ached.

"What do you have, Nuge?"

"We found something he said twice, the last time you two talked. He said it once about himself and once about you."

"Tell me."

"He said it would be his 'most beautiful move' and he said the moves you made were 'most beautiful'. It sounded strange and it triggered Nicky's memory about something she read while doing research for a thesis back in college. There is a chess match from 1912 actually known as "the most beautiful move'".

"Go on." Worton said, his anxiety growing by the minute.

"It was a game between American Frank Marshall and Russian Stefan Lewitzky." Nuge said. He listened to moments of silence on the other end of the line before Worton spoke again.

"Frank Lewitzky. The name he has been using all along".

"Exactly." Nuge said.

Worton's mind raced, trying to calculate the new information and what it meant.

"Do we know what part of the city this game would be situated in on our chessboard?"

"Yes. We believe it is the square just above you somewhere between 42nd and 34th Streets and 2nd and 3rd Avenues." Nuge said. "That is the square Frank Marshall moved to during his 1912 match. He called it his "most beautiful move". Experts have called it the greatest single move of all time in championship match play."

Worton tried to relax and think.

"Okay. He may have already acted or that may be his decoy to throw us off. I'm staying here until we know a possible sight, or victim, other than Menchenko. Do we have a list of possibilities in this ten-block area?"

"Close, we are still working on that," Nuge said. "But here's the kicker. In this 1912 game, Marshall put his queen at risk, not his king, forcing Lewitzky to exchange queen for queen. He went on to win the game in five more moves. Paul, we're convinced he's after a queen and not a king".

Paul Worton did not answer. He sat staring at the chess board by his side holding the phone to his ear.

"Paul, are you there?" Nuge finally asked.

"Nuge, put Morales on now!" Worton said.

"Yeah, Paul, what do you think?" Morales asked.

"Jose, don't let Nicky out of your sight. She does not leave the precinct without you. Do you understand? This bastard already got Anthony. He's not getting Nicky too. And get me that list of sights".

Paul Worton hung up before Morales could answer. He punched a number on his phone. "Dispatch, this is Detective Paul Worton. I need you to contact the detail watching my house and the detail at my wife's store. I am keeping this line open. I need you to do it now."

It seemed like an eternity before the dispatcher's voice crackled in his phone.

"Detective Worton? I'm sorry but no one is answering my call at either site. I will report...."

Worton pressed 'end' to shut her off before she finished and punched the number "1" on his speed dial. Three rings later, Lori's co-worker answered.

"Hello." Melanie said.

"Mel, let me talk to Lori." He barked.

"Oh, hi Paul, she left for the day. She must have forgotten her phone – it was here under some papers when it rang."

Worton's heart sank.

"Did she say where she was going?" He asked.

"Yeah, to Jackie's game."

Worton tried to focus.

"Anything weird happen before she left? Did she say anything else?"

"No. She gave me some paperwork to ship some stuff for some European guy and then left. He offered to walk her out." Worton could hardly breathe."

"Do you have a name? What did he buy?" Worton asked.

"Let's see. The invoice is right here. Oops, hold on, something fell. Sorry, a ring was under the papers and it fell."

"A ring?" Worton asked. "What kind of ring?"

"It looks like a class ring or something. No wait. It says 1972 Champions with a number 15 and the initials PW."

Worton tried to think. His heart was racing. .

"Mel, this is very important. Did she say anything about where she was going?"

"Well, she said she was going to Jackie's game and then she left with that man. Is everything alright?" She asked.

Worton didn't answer. He hung up and started punching numbers on his phone. The voice on the other end answered.

"Copeland here, what's up Paul?"

"He played us Tim. He has Lori, and maybe Jackie. I need you to get Emergency Service to my house as fast as possible. He may not be coming here at all, or they may be trade bait so he can get to Menchenko. Tim, I have to know about Jackie before I make another move."

"I'm on my way." Copeland said. The line went dead.

* * *

Andy Wiley dozed in his swivel chair. He had been trying to stay awake but for the last hour, his chin would inadvertently drop to his chest and wake him with a start. Each time, he rubbed his eyes, shook his head and checked his computer. The same flashing light kept blinking back at him.

'be patient'... 'be patient'

Andy sighed. Seven o'clock. This was cutting it close: only five hours to go. But Mueller had come through every time. He had not failed him yet. As he stretched and leaned back in his chair, his office door opened. Lori Worton and Michael Mueller walked in. Wiley almost fell over backwards as he tried to right himself.

"Excuse me. Who are you? Our offices are closed. You can't barge in here without knocking." He exclaimed.

"Be very quiet, Mr. Wiley. I told you to wait here for me, and you have. Now, if you do as I say, your patience will be rewarded." Mueller said.

Andy Wiley's eyes were wide and his mouth hung open – almost in a comical state.

"You are Michael Mueller?"

"Yes, I am. And this is Mrs. Lori Worton." Mueller said as he locked the office door.

"But I was waiting for a message." a confused Wiley said pointing to his computer.

"I never said there would be a message. I only told you to be here from 12:01 a.m. to 12-midnight on September 1st. You were to get an exclusive on the final game of this great chess match," Mueller said. "And you shall. Now, please be seated Mrs. Worton."

Lori did not speak. For the most part, she said nothing from the time they left the store and took a taxi up 3rd Avenue, to the corner of 42nd Street. They had walked calmly down 42nd Street, hand-in-hand, as Mueller insisted, like any other tourist couple in the city. He had pulled her close to the back of the *Daily News* building, as if in a loving embrace. As he leaned into her, he used a brass key to unlock a door immediately behind them. Once inside, they made their way to the fire stairs and quickly up to the fourth floor. They did not encounter a soul.

Lori sat in the chair as instructed. She was determined to do as he said, as long as she believed her daughter would not be harmed.

"What do you propose?" Wiley asked. He was scared. Seeing Mueller in person had never crossed his mind. He was fine reporting the horrors of other people's lives, but in the real world, Andy Wiley was a very weak man who shied away from any confrontation – verbal or physical. He thought he might throw up in front of this man.

"You need do nothing but remember the events of the next two hours and report what you see," Mueller said. "You will see my final triumph over Detective Worton and the New York Police Department. You will see me finish the most brilliant chess move of all time: confounding my opponents to the point they do not even know which piece is being attacked. You will see, and you will report for all the world, that Michael Mueller played the ultimate game of chess and won."

Lori Worton laughed out loud and both men stared at her.

"Are you serious," she asked. "You'll be remembered as a murderer and nothing else. Son of Sam, Jeffrey Daumer, PTK, Boston Strangler. A killer. Not a chess player. Don't kid yourself. This is no game. No one is going to say you're a great chess player. Fischer, Kasparov, Spassky. Those guys are chess players. And then there's you - Michael Mueller. You'll be the "Chess Board Serial Killer", not a world-renowned chess player."

Wiley was silent, staring from the killer to the defiant woman looking up at him.

"You are much like your husband, Mrs. Worton. Smart, confident and capable, but do not provoke me." Mueller warned.

Lori laughed again at the man towering over her.

"Why not? Should I worry that you might hurt me?" She asked sarcastically. "I'm obviously your last victim. The kid here is simply a pawn to get the publicity out. You chose me to put the final touches on your ridiculous attempt to create a chess game against Paul and the Police Department. Make no mistake somehow some way, they will catch you. Sooner or later the headlines will read, 'police capture a crazed serial killer.'"

Mueller was angry and red in the face. His neck muscles were bulging and he had to pull from inside to quell his emotions. Still, he spoke with an edge in his voice.

"Have you forgotten about your daughter?"

"No, but you can't harm her now. If she's alive and well now, she'll stay that way. It's me you want." She said defiantly.

Mueller watched her for a moment, a long admiring moment.

"You may just be as dangerous as your husband. It is just after seven now. In about forty-five minutes they will close the lobby to the public and lock the front doors. We will wait a few hours to make sure we are not disturbed, so you might as well make yourselves comfortable."

* * *

Paul Worton had been in many tight spots over his twenty-five years on the force, but never had he felt so helpless. He could not leave Victor Menchenko until he knew Mueller's next move. Menchenko's address and name were on the wall in Mueller's apartment. As far as Worton knew, Menchenko was still the target. Was he using Lori as bait to get to Menchenko or was it one of Mueller's brilliant tactics to throw them off? The move of a chess piece on a chess board to fool an opponent.

Worton answered his cell-phone on the first ring.

"Worton here."

"Paul. It's Copeland. I'm at your house. Jackie is here but there is no sign of Lori," Copeland said. Worton tried to control his emotions before he spoke.

"Is Jackie okay?"

"Yeah, he must have drugged her, but he didn't hurt her. She was asleep in her room. The EMT's gave her something to wake her and they are with her now. She is drowsy. The last thing she remembers is reading her book and sun-bathing in the backyard." Copeland said.

"She never heard from her mom? Never saw anything?" Worton asked.

"No, nothing. We're taking statements from Carson and Michaels. We found them on the next street over, where they had a good view of the front of your house. Of course Carson was asleep and Michaels had his head buried in a video Game Boy. They were the most surprised people on the street when we stormed the place." Copeland was spitting the words in disgust at this point. "If they get another assignment, and that is a big "if", it will be as a uniform walking a beat in Harlem. We figure

Mueller just skirted our guys and approached from the back of the house."

"Thanks, Boss," Worton said. "Do a favor for me Tim? Make sure she's protected until this is over."

"You got it," Copeland said. "What is your next plan of action?"

"Morales and Walsh are at the store. It seems the two guys covering Lori were a bit tired of the job, too. Mueller stuck a rag in their tailpipe while they were napping. Johnson is in the hospital and his partner is back at the House waiting to be debriefed," Worton said. "My next move is to call Morales and see if they found anything. We have two hours left and I am not leaving until I know Mueller is not coming here. I really don't know what else to do."

"Okay Paul, don't worry. Lori will be fine. He wants Menchenko. He is just trying to throw us off. Keep me updated." Copeland said.

The phone went dead.

Paul Worton hit two on his speed dial. Detective Morales answered on the first ring.

"Morales here."

"Jose. Jackie is fine and Copeland is with her but no sign of Lori," Worton said. "Anything new there?"

"No, we've checked everything. We have the ring, the signed paperwork and statements from all the employees, but the only one Lori and Mueller talked to was Melanie Bailey." Morales said.

"Tell me everything she said."

"It seems Melanie Bailey talked to Mueller first about a month ago. He ordered some stuff and then came back today to have the stuff shipped. But he asked to speak to the manager first," Morales said, continuing to read from his notes. "When she saw Lori again, Mueller was with her. Lori had the paperwork to ship Mueller's stuff and she told Miss Bailey she was leaving for the day." Morales said.

"Did she say anything else?" Worton asked. Morales checked his notes once more.

"Not much here. Just that she was going to Jackie's game and probably taking the girls to some ice cream place, called Teresa's on the way home. That was it." Morales said.

"Teresa's? There's no Teresa's ice cream place on the way home from the ball field to my house. There is no Teresa's in the whole damn town." Worton said.

The line went dead before Detective Morales could comment.

* * *

Four hours had passed when Michael Mueller stood and walked to the desk where Andy Wiley sat dozing with his head resting on his folded arms. He did not have to wake Lori Worton. Her eyes had not left him from the moment they entered the room. Mueller jabbed the young reporter in the shoulder with the small .32 caliber Beretta he held in his hand.

"Mr. Wiley, get your camera and a notebook. It is time to begin the 'End Game' of this match." Mueller said.

To emphasize, he waved the weapon toward the office door .

"Let's retire to the lobby, shall we?" He said.

* * *

The lower level, inner workings, of the *Daily News* building are as busy as a beehive twenty-four hours a day seven days a week. But the front entrance is more of a tourist attraction than anything else. It is used by sightseers, corporate types and certain employees who use it as a shortcut to elevators for a quick ride to the working offices below.

Now, the lobby of the *Daily News* building was deserted and dimly lit. The front entrance closed every evening, at eight sharp, to everyone but the janitor and Mueller had eliminated any chance of the old man interrupting them. The recessed ceiling and floor lights left a ghostly glow along the time zone clocks lining the far left wall. Andy Wiley was terrified. Not for his safety, but for what he was about to witness. His arms were free but he was buckled, with a leather strap around his waist and a padlock, to the bronze railing facing the clocks along the wall. Mueller had placed the notebook and pencil in Wiley's shirt pocket and his 35 mm camera was in his hand. Mueller made it clear that Wiley would either document what he saw, or become a victim himself. What he saw turned his stomach.

Lori Worton fought Michael Mueller but, in the end, she was no match for the stronger man. After some difficulty, he had subdued her. She stood on tiptoes, hands tied high above her head, with a rope thrown over a ceiling pipe. Mueller cut her blouse away, leaving her only in jeans and her bra. Mueller had activated a tape recorder attached to his waist and continued to narrate his actions into the mouthpiece.

"Photos, Mr. Wiley. Photos." He instructed. With shaking hands, Andy Wiley reeled off a series of snapshots.

"This will be the culmination of my life's work. You will not hear from me again. In the *End Game*, I have followed a strategy that has completely baffled my opponents. It was vintage Bobby Fischer, leaving my opponents dumbfounded and destroyed. Now it is time to complete the task".

Mueller stepped behind Lori and pulled a long, thin 8-inch knife from the scabbard inside his jacket. He slid his hand down her skin, along her right side, until he found the spot he wanted.

"It is a bit of an irony that you will feel the same steel as young Detective Austin. I know you were close," Mueller whispered. "Here, between your fourth and fifth rib, lies a direct line to your liver. I am not cruel. I will make the thrust quick and final. You will not die instantly, but will bleed out within twenty minutes."

"Any last words, Mrs. Worton?" Mueller asked.

Lori cringed at his touch. Tears welled in her eyes but she looked defiantly at the camera.

"Wiley. You tell my husband and my daughter, I love them. And then, tell my husband to get this sick bastard." She said.

"You can tell me yourself, Baby. I'm right here." Paul Worton said.

Mueller, Lori and Andy Wiley's heads all snapped around to see Paul Worton step out of the shadows of the front entrance to the building. His Smith & Wesson was trained on the middle of Lori's chest. Her body acted as a shield for Mueller, depriving Paul of a direct shot at the killer. Wiley shouted.

"Do something!"

"Shut up!" Worton said.

Lori's eyes fixed on Paul. He would have a plan. She tried to train her mind back to her days on the job, waiting for some sign from her husband.

"Oh my God," Mueller laughed. "I never would have believed you could get to this point. You are a genius. You could be a world class player yourself." He moved even closer to Lori, wrapping one arm around her waist and bringing the knife to her throat.

"I'm a cop, nothing else, and I'm being helped by a thousand other cops when dealing with the likes of you. They figured out your play. Now let her go. It's over. You lose."

"Oh no. She leaves with me. You give the order and I go free. Stalemate. Not the best scenario, but I can live with it. After I am safe, I let her go and I tell you where your daughter is."

"We already found Jackie at home. And she's fine,"

Lori sobbed but kept her eyes on her husband.

"Ah, well, she was never in danger, but I needed to convince your lovely wife to accompany me," Mueller said. "You made it much tougher by putting your detectives in my way. But I love a challenge. In this game, you must be ready to change tactics at any moment. You will be relieved to know that I did them no permanent damage."

"We have Jackie and my men are being cared for. Now let her go. No one else gets hurt here."

"No. No. You should know by now that I'm not stupid. She must go with me." As he spoke, Mueller sliced the rope binding Lori's hands, but quickly brought the knife back to her neck.

"Remember our illustrious conductor at Carnegie Hall? Or even better, young Anthony. One move of this knife and you will have killed your own wife, Detective."

Andy Wiley was now in full media form. He had forgotten fear and was filming everything he could. There had never been a news event like this filmed and he was the reporter.

Mueller eased Lori away from the clocks and toward the wall behind the huge globe. Worton braced his feet again with each step, never taking the sight of his weapon away from his target. The problem was, Mueller had Lori between them.

"Look. I came in here to try to reason with you. You can't get out without getting caught. This place is surrounded." Worton said.

"You can get me out. Now, lower your weapon and we will leave together. All three of us," Mueller said. "Like I said before... Stalemate."

Worton lowered his weapon and Mueller smiled.

"Very good Detective, you really have no choice."

"Okay. You win. Just be careful with that knife. How do I know you will let her go?"

Lori tried to concentrate on Paul's every word. She knew he was trying to tell her something. He would never let Mueller go.

Wiley kept snapping pictures. He would write the story later. But, for now, he wanted to document every move of the confrontation. He made a mental note of the exact moment Detective Worton decided to barter with Mueller.

"Listen. I know, and you know, that you are not vulnerable as long as you have her in that position. We cannot get at you as long as you are using her as a shield. But you can't go out that front door because I'm standing right here."

Worton spoke again.

"And you can't go to your right because Detective Morales is there." As he spoke, Jose Morales stepped into the dim light with his 9 mm trained on the suspect.

"And you can't go to your left."

Nicky Walsh moved out from the corridor to Mueller's left in a classic firing range stance, weapon at the ready.

Mueller looked from one police officer to the other and back to Worton.

"We've got you from all angles Mueller. All we need is for you to move."

Suddenly, Lori knew what he was telling her. Now she waited for his signal. The only sound in the room was the sound of Andy Wiley's camera, as Mueller and Worton stared at each other. The tip of the long blade inched closer, almost breaking the skin.

"I will kill her." Mueller said, in a deadly whisper.

Worton brought his weapon back to a firing position, trained on his wife's chest. Their eyes locked. Worton winked and Lori smiled. It was the signal she was waiting for.

She slammed the heel of her right shoe, as hard as she could, on Mueller's right foot. At the same time, she drove her left elbow back into his ribs. The knife at her throat moved no more than an inch and Mueller's body twisted no more than half a turn, exposing his right shoulder and upper chest, only for an instant.

It was enough.

Three bullets ripped into Michael Mueller's body at almost the same instant. Nicky Walsh's bullet hit Mueller's left knee buckling his leg and loosening his grip on Lori. The moment the knife moved, Jose Morales fired, shattering Mueller's right hand, sending the knife over the railing to the floor below and showering Lori's face with blood.

Finally, Paul Worton's shot hit Mueller in the upper right chest the moment Lori's movement gave him a shot.

Mueller collapsed against the wall and slid to a sitting position. Lori slumped to the floor next to the brass railing. Paul was on one knee next to her before she could move. He pulled her to him. The shots continued to echo in the room, leaving everyone partially deaf.

"Are you okay?" He shouted. "You're not hit are you?"

"No." She sobbed into his chest.

He pulled his jacket off to cover her and wiped her face off with the sleeve.

"You are one cool cookie, Baby. Glad you remembered your training." He said, kissing her lips.

"Cool? I'm shaking like a leaf," she said. "Is Jackie okay? Where is she?"

"She's home and safe. Copeland left a detail there and your sister is with her. Mueller gave her something. She was out cold in her bed when Emergency Services got there. Fire and Rescue had to revive her, but she is fine now."

"They found Carson and Michaels lounging in their car. They were half-assed watching the front of the house while Mueller was sneaking up on Jackie sunning in the backyard. Copeland is getting their statements. The guys covering you are a different story. Seems they got bored with the job and were asleep in the vehicle behind the store with the motor running. Mueller stuffed something in the tailpipe and the carbon monoxide nearly killed them. Johnson is in the hospital and his partner is at the precinct trying to answer Copeland's questions."

Lori wrapped her arms around her husband's neck and hung on as tight as she 1could.

"Thank God you got here in time." Lori said.

"That's all you're doing Baby. You left the ring, so I would know Jackie was in danger, and mentioning *TERESA'S* was brilliant," Paul said. "Thankfully someone with the task force knew *TERESA'S* was the restaurant here at the *Daily News* building"

"Hey, someone let me out of this".

Andy Wiley was still strapped to the railing. He held the camera in one hand, while trying to release himself with the other. Paul ignored Wiley and turned his attention to Michael Mueller. Nicky Walsh still had her weapon trained on the wounded man as Morales spoke into his radio.

"Ten-thirteen, officers need assistance, shots fired, suspect, down. We need a bus and a supervisor. No other casualties."

"Jose, release Wiley, but keep him here," Worton asked. "Nicky, can you help Lori?"

Worton knelt in front of Michael Mueller. Mueller's eyes were squeezed shut in pain. His face was pale and he was losing a lot of blood. He looked up at Worton.

"You are a revelation, Detective. I never thought you could find me here."

"You almost had me Mueller, but luckily an old chess player and a young chess player figured out your 'most beautiful move'. Then we just had to get here in time," Worton replied. "You can thank my wife for that."

Mueller grimaced.

"The 'End Game' is sometimes brutal, Detective," Mueller said. "You win."

"Checkmate." Worton said as Mueller closed his eyes and slumped against the wall.

Worton walked across the lobby of the *Daily News* building as Crime Scene and EMT's swarmed in the door. He walked directly to Andy Wiley and Jose Morales. He grabbed the reporter by the arm and pulled him into a dark alcove. Detective Morales shielded the corner. Worton ripped the camera from Wiley's hands, popped the back open and tore the film out. Wiley screamed.

"What are you doing?"

Worton grabbed him by the throat.

"Shut up you sniveling parasite. I've wanted to kick your ass since this started. You have done nothing but add fuel to this city's fear and I know you will be on the air tomorrow with more of the same," Worton spat the words out. "But no one is going to see those pictures of my wife and Mueller, and don't bother sending anyone for interviews from me or my family."

Worton released his grip and started to walk away.

"You are worse than Mueller. He's a psycho. You just don't care who you hurt as long as it gets you ahead."

He left Andy Wiley in the corner, staring at the torn film lying at his feet.

* * *

EPILOGUE

November 1st broke cool and crisp over New York City. The leaves were starting to turn out over the Island and the Halloween festivities had given way to Thanksgiving preparations. Michael Mueller would spend the rest of his holidays in maximum security. He had been charged with six counts of pre-meditated murder and was looking at no chance of parole. He would spend those years with a deformed right hand and a pronounced limp.

Tim Copeland had deferred all accolades to the detectives working under him. The Bosses, who were calling for his head only days before, wanted to move him to a position in the Commissioner's Office, but he refused. He belonged in the 18th Precinct house, working day-to-day, with his detectives.

The entire task force received a commendation from the department for a job well done. Jose Morales received a citation from the city for his actions during the 'Chess Board Murder' investigations, while Officer Nicky Walsh was decorated and promoted to Detective 3rd class, and assigned to the 18th Precinct Detective Squad.

Jackie was happy again. Her parents were back to a fairly normal life and she was thrilled to be back at school with her friends. She was the only freshman on the high school volleyball team which was heading to the playoffs for the first time in five years.

The King's Gambit

Andy Wiley's description of the standoff at the *Daily News* building hit every news outlet across the world. He had his book deal and was sending out feelers for a Hollywood movie. He had his wish. He was a media star from coast-to-coast. He would move to California soon. He was not well-liked by NYPD and figured things would be easier out there.

Paul Worton got a month's vacation time, on the books, from the department. He and Lori spent a long weekend at the beach house and then relaxed around the house, spending as much time as possible with Jackie.

Victor Menchenko was in the news. He was the subject of magazine and newspaper reports, asking for an analysis of how Mueller's actions fit in with the game of chess. They wanted to know about his relationship with the killer and his family. Finally, they wanted to know if Menchenko believed Mueller was truly a great chess player.

"The Nuge" was back to his normal routine of tennis, racquetball, chess and aggravating everyone he knew. He was pretty proud of himself and never tired of telling Paul how he had cracked the case.

On this Monday, two months after Mueller's capture, Paul Worton maneuvered his car onto the Brooklyn Bridge and into traffic that was heavy, but not brutal. He was at this very spot when Tim Copeland called him on July 12th to report a murder at Carnegie Hall. He remembered looking out at the empty skyline where the Twin Towers once stood, remembering the heroes who had died.

Now, he glanced at the plaque in the passenger seat next to him. Anthony Austin's citation had been presented posthumously. Before they left the city, Anthony's parents asked Paul to take the plaque and put it up in a place where Anthony would be remembered by his fellow detectives. Paul would stop by the Academy Training Facility that Anthony loved so much, and hang it on the gym wall so that all recruits would forever remember a fallen officer killed in the line of duty. What better role model than Anthony for a recruit just entering the Police Academy Training Center?

Paul Worton looked once more across the river to the empty skyline at the tip of Manhattan. From this moment on, he would have one more hero to remember.

ACKNOWLEDGMENTS

I would like to thank some very important people who helped make this book possible.

First, to two men I have never met. Richard Roberts wrote *Fischer/Spassky The New York Times Report on the Chess Match of the Century* and, though I was alive and infatuated with the Fischer/Spassky match, his telling of the story gave me an insight to a time in history that I found invaluable. In 1972, I sat in front of my television set every night and watched a man on PBS television tell the world what was happening, a world away in Iceland. That man was chess master Shelby Lyman. His quotes and writings on chess were an enormous help and gave me a much better understanding of the game itself and a better ability to tell my story.

I have to thank my brother-in-law, Reid since I am as computer illiterate as is humanly possible for a writer. Without his help, numerous times, this book would be lost somewhere in cyberspace.

To Bob and Mary, who spent a long weekend with me walking the chessboard of New York City in search of ten appropriate squares to checkmate a "King". To my brothers, Bob and Tim, my longtime and closest friend Charlene, Manny (Maestro) Cruz and my octogenarian good buddy, Robert Nugent (the real

Nooge), who combined to serve as my sounding board with praise, encouragement and crucial, constructive criticism.

To Tim Copeland, my friend and retired New York City homicide detective, for his willingness to share a wealth of knowledge about the inner workings of a high profile homicide investigation and police work in general and to Dean, my buddy and fellow writer, for his weapons expertise and friendship.

Last to Barb, my wife of thirty-eight years, for being the inspiration in everything I do well, and for saying yes.

ABOUT THE AUTHOR

Tom Blenk is a retired postal worker from New Hampshire living in North Carolina. He started writing in 1999 and published his first book, *"The Ridge"* two years later. He has written a magazine article on local WWII veterans in his area and is currently working on a third novel. Please visit his website at www.booksbytomblenk.com